DATE DUE

DEMCO 38-296

THE SQUARE ROOT

of WONDERFUL

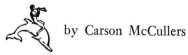 by Carson McCullers

THE HEART IS A LONELY HUNTER

REFLECTIONS IN A GOLDEN EYE

THE MEMBER OF THE WEDDING

THE BALLAD OF THE SAD CAFÉ

THE SQUARE ROOT OF WONDERFUL

The Square Root of *Wonderful*

A Play by Carson McCullers

Cherokee Publishing Company
Atlanta, Georgia
1990

in-Publication Data

The square root of wonderful

: a play / by Carson McCullers.

p.   cm.

Reprint. Originally published : Boston : Houghton Mifflin, 1958.
ISBN 0-87797-188-9 (cloth) : $17.95
1. Title.
PS3525.A1772S63   1990

812'.52--dc20   90-47728
                                                                 CIP

This book is printed on acid-free paper which conforms to the American
National Standard Z39.48-1984 *Permanence of Paper for Printed Library
Materials.* Paper that conforms to this standard's requirements for pH,
alkaline reserve and freedom from groundwood is anticipated to last
several hundred years without significant deterioration under normal
library use and storage conditions.

Manufactured in the United States of America

ISBN: 0-87797-188-9

94   93   92   91   90   10   9   8   7   6   5   4   3   2   1

Published by arrangement with Houghton Mifflin Company.

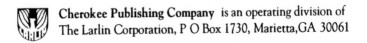 Cherokee Publishing Company is an operating division of
The Larlin Corporation, P O Box 1730, Marietta, GA 30061

The Square Root of Wonderful was first presented by Saint-Subber and Figaro, Inc., at the National Theater, New York City, on October 30, 1957.

CAST (*in order of appearance*)

PARIS LOVEJOY	*Kevin Coughlin*
MOLLIE LOVEJOY	*Anne Baxter*
JOHN TUCKER	*Philip Abbott*
LOREENA LOVEJOY	*Martine Bartlett*
MOTHER LOVEJOY	*Jean Dixon*
PHILLIP LOVEJOY	*William Smithers*
JOEY BARNES	*Kippy Campbell*

Directed by GEORGE KEATHLEY
Scenery and lighting by JO MIELZINER
Costumes by NOEL TAYLOR

A Personal Preface

MANY PEOPLE have asked me why I like writing for the theatre. I wrote *The Member of the Wedding* first as a book and it took me five years. Once the novel was finished I had that happy, depleted feeling a writer has after finishing a long stretch of work. I had no notion at the time that I would dramatize it. Then Tennessee Williams wrote me about the book and asked me if I would come and spend the summer with him on Nantucket and I accepted the invitation.

During that sea-summer lit with the glow of a new friendship (we had not met before and had known each other only through our work) he suggested I do *The Member of the Wedding* as a play.

I was hesitant at first, knowing nothing about the theatre. I had seen only about ten plays in my life, including high school *Hamlets* and *Vagabond Kings*, but the visual and dramatic aspects of the novel I had written compelled me. Tennessee borrowed a typewriter for me and we settled down to the same dining table. He was working on *Summer and Smoke* while I began the play version of *The Member of the Wedding*. We would work from ten to two and then go to the beach on sunny days or read poetry aloud when it rained. Tennessee and I have spent many ocean-summers since and our friendship is a continuing joy and inspiration to me.

Despite forecasts of disaster the vitality and truth of the

viii – A Personal Preface

play, magnificently produced and performed was immediately appreciated. My own financial problems were solved and, most important, I fell in love with the theatre. The play was a new and radiant creative experience to me.

When people ask why I write for the theatre I can only counter with another question. Why does anyone write at all? I suppose a writer writes out of some inward compulsion to transform his own experience (much of it is unconscious) into the universal and symbolical. The themes the artist chooses are always deeply personal. I suppose my central theme is the theme of spiritual isolation. Certainly I have always felt alone. In addition to being lonely, a writer is also amorphous. A writer soon discovers he has no single identity but lives the lives of all the people he creates and his weathers are independent of the actual day around him. I live with the people I create and it has always made my essential loneliness less keen.

In *The Square Root of Wonderful* I recognize many of the compulsions that made me write this play. My husband wanted to be a writer and his failure in that was one of the disappointments that led to his death. When I started *The Square Root of Wonderful* my mother was very ill and after a few months she died. I wanted to re-create my mother — to remember her tranquil beauty and sense of joy in life. So, unconsciously, the life-death theme of *The Square Root of Wonderful* emerged.

Present-day audiences have been accustomed to plays that have a single emotional direction. If it's a modern tragedy the overtones of tragedy are undisturbed by the comedy of the every day. In the modern comedy such themes as death and failure are so subordinated that they are almost inexistent. Yet audiences do respond to tragi-comedy when the absurd and painful truths of life are combined in a single line.

I was aware of the risk in alternating comic and tragic

scenes, aware that it confuses the same audience who can respond readily to a single situation with both laughter and tears. This is mostly true in the theatre; a reader of novels is more emotionally flexible because he has the time to reflect before he is pushed on to the next action.

Writing a play can be among the most satisfying experiences of an author's life. If he is lucky, the production, with the constellation of artists involved, can heighten and give the fullest dimension to the script and the audience serves to intensify the experience and to make the author feel yes, that's it. That's just what I had in mind — and more. The author is rarely so lucky. There are pressures of the theatre — the deadlines, the last-minute decisions and changes that are nerve-breaking for a writer. For the theatre is a most pragmatical art, and if a scene does not work it has to be altered.

I have learned this in my work in the theatre: the author must work alone until the intentions of his play are fulfilled — until the play is as finished as the author can make it. Once a play is in rehearsal, a playwright must write under unaccustomed pressure, and alas, what he had in mind is often compromised. This may be due to the actors, the producer, the director — the whole prism of the theatrical production.

And so begins a transmutation that sometimes to the author's dismay ends in the play being almost unrecognizable to the creator.

That is why of the five or six evolutions this play went through I prefer to publish the one which follows. It is the last one I wrote before the production was set in motion and is the most nearly the truth of what I want to say in *The Square Root of Wonderful.*

Many novelists have been attracted to the theatre — Fitzgerald, Wolfe, James and Joyce. Perhaps this is because of the loneliness of a writer's life — the unaccustomed joy of participating creatively with others is marvelous to a writer. It is rare that a writer is equally skilled as a novelist and a playwright. I don't want to open this can of beans, but I would say simply that the writer is compelled to write, and the form is determined by some veiled inward need that perhaps the writer himself does not fully understand.

I want to thank Jo Mielziner, Arnold Saint-Subber, Robert Lanz, Joseph Mankiewicz and George Keathley for their very able and talented contributions to *The Square Root of Wonderful*.

Carson McCullers

CAST OF CHARACTERS

PARIS LOVEJOY
                Son of Mollie and Phillip Lovejoy
MOLLIE LOVEJOY   *a beautiful young woman*
JOHN TUCKER   *an architect*
LOREENA LOVEJOY   *Phillip Lovejoy's sister*
MOTHER LOVEJOY   *Phillip Lovejoy's mother*
PHILLIP LOVEJOY   *the husband of Mollie*
HATTIE BROWN   *a friend of Paris*

TIME: The present

ACT I: A May midnight
ACT II: The next afternoon
ACT III: Scene 1: Just before dawn of the following day
           Scene 2: A week later

THE SQUARE ROOT

of WONDERFUL

ACT I

Time: A May midnight.

Scene: Living room of a comfortable house twenty miles from New York. A small apple farm. The room is comfortable, unpretentious, homey. There is a door upstage center leading to the outside with window seats on either side. When the door is open we see a branch of apple blossoms from the grandfather clock at the foot of the stairway. The stairway, stage left, leads to a shallow landing and two bedrooms upstairs.

Stage left we see a small pantry leading to a kitchen. A door downstage right leads to a small sewing room. There is a sofa and a few pieces of furniture, homey, with a faint air of elegance, but homey.

At Rise: At curtain rise the stage is dark except for a crack of light under the door of the kitchen. We hear gurgle nightmare sounds. MOLLIE enters from kitchen, followed a little later by JOHN. When MOLLIE turns on light we see PARIS asleep on the sofa.

MOLLIE

You are having a nightmare. Wake up, darling.

PARIS

Where am I?

MOLLIE

Safe in your mother's arms.

PARIS

Oh! It was awful.

JOHN
What was it, Paris?

PARIS
I dreamed a burglar was in the house. A dark man in a kind of burglar's cap — at first I didn't see his face.

MOLLIE
It was just a nightmare. There's not any burglar here.

PARIS
And the moonlight. When I saw the burglar's face. It was so strange — so awful.

MOLLIE
I was afraid that lamb curry was too rich.

PARIS
The door opened like a hinged window. You know how queer dream windows are. And I was trying to scream, to warn you. And when I saw the burglar's face it was —

MOLLIE
All this rich food.

PARIS
The burglar was my father — in a burglar's cap.

MOLLIE
Silly-billy! You see how silly the whole thing is. There's no burglar in the house and it's past two o'clock.

PARIS
Why are you up so late?

MOLLIE
We were drinking tea in the kitchen and talking.

PARIS
What were you talking about? Not that I'm nosey or anything like that.

MOLLIE
We were talking about San Francisco and mousetraps. John
set the trap for that mouse.

PARIS
Why were you talking about San Francisco?

MOLLIE
John is leaving us soon. He has a job there. I will be desolate
without him.

JOHN
Will you, Mollie?

MOLLIE
Yes. Quite lost, in fact.

(JOHN *gently puts his arms around Mollie.*)

PARIS
Why, John?

JOHN
Why what?

PARIS
Why do you put your arms around my mother? Why do
you look at her that way?

JOHN
What way?

PARIS
When you look at her, your eyes are zany.

MOLLIE
Don't be fractious, Lambie. It unhinges me.

JOHN
Go to sleep, Paris. Your mother is tired, unhinged.

MOLLIE
Yes, when I looked in the mirror today I had nine gray hairs.

PARIS
Why do you keep your arms around my mother? Why do you look at her in that zany way?

JOHN
Because I love your mother.

PARIS
You can't love my mother. She's my mother. She married my father not only once but twice.

JOHN
But now she's divorced.

PARIS
That makes no difference. You've only known her for ten days.

JOHN

The Russian Revolution took place in just ten days, and love can happen in an hour, even sometimes at first sight.

PARIS

I used to like you O.K. I used to like you swell. But now I don't know. When you first came, I was glad to have another man in the house. But now I wonder what my father would think.

MOLLIE

Your father's been away more than a year, Lambie and now we're divorced.

PARIS

But he telephoned you.

JOHN

Did he, Mollie?

MOLLIE

Only when he was under the influence. You know what I mean?

JOHN

I know.

PARIS

You always said Daddy was coming back.

MOLLIE

I always thought so, but now I'm afraid so.

PARIS

I'm going to tell my father what John said.

JOHN
If I ever see him, I'll tell him myself.

PARIS
My father is the greatest writer in the world. Phillip Lovejoy, author of *The Chinaberry Tree* and *The Prison of Air*, look him up in *Who's Who*.

MOLLIE
It's true, your father's a genius.

PARIS
My father's a man nobody can fool around with.

MOLLIE
Don't shout so, Lambie, you'll wake up Mother Lovejoy and Sister, and they're exhausted after their trip.

PARIS
Let them wake up. I'll tell Granny what John said too.

JOHN
Tell her.

PARIS
To me love is a big fake. You can't eat it.

MOLLIE
Don't be cynical, Paris.

PARIS
I'm not cynical, I'm starved.

MOLLIE
Nightmares. Stuffing yourself all day. Starved indeed.

PARIS
Anyway, I can't sleep on this scroungy sofa.

MOLLIE
With Mother Lovejoy and Sister here, we just have to make do.

PARIS
Why did Granny and Auntie Sister come?

MOLLIE
They've come to visit us and see your father's play.

PARIS
His play opened and closed a month ago.

MOLLIE
Don't talk about it, Lambie. It's a sore subject.

PARIS
I'll finish the night in the library. That sofa's bigger, I think.

MOLLIE
Nighty-night, Lambie.

JOHN
Sleep tight.

PARIS
To me love is goofy. Good night, you all.

(PARIS *exits with bedcovers.*)

JOHN
What do you say, Mollie?

MOLLIE
I honestly don't know what to say. You never told me you loved me before.

JOHN
Did I need to?

MOLLIE
No, there's a certain light in your eye and your voice. But to tell it the first time in front of Paris. When did it start?

JOHN
The April afternoon ten days ago when we first met. The afternoon my life was altered. Why did you pick me up?

MOLLIE
The day was so lovely. You had on a leather jacket and you were carrying a monkey wrench. I think anybody carrying a monkey wrench on a lonely road is so handsome.

JOHN
My car had broken down.

MOLLIE
You looked so lonely on that lonesome road. I just wanted to chat a while, so I stopped the car and asked if I could give you a lift.

JOHN
It was such a lovely afternoon.

MOLLIE

I took you home, without thinking or asking.

JOHN

Why did you?

MOLLIE

It was the day that Paris was away on the Independency Hike, and I felt lonesome and unprotected.

JOHN

You told me it was the first time you had spent a night away from your child.

MOLLIE

That's right. I had wanted to go along as a sort of Scout mother. But Paris was furious at the very suggestion.

JOHN

These Scout hikes are very independent. They don't even use matches. They whittle sticks.

MOLLIE

A mother feels so uncared for and unprotected — the first night her child is away.

JOHN

So because you felt unprotected, you pick up a total stranger and take him home. Mollie, do you know what could have happened?

MOLLIE

You didn't feel like a total stranger.

JOHN

I might have stolen the Lovejoy silver. I might have been a
madman who played creepy music on the zither in the middle
of the night. I might have been a sex maniac — I might have
ravished you — violated you — and strangled you with a —
whatever they use. You say you felt scared and unprotected
— and yet you pick up the first man you see on the road and
bring him home with you.

MOLLIE

I was missing my husband and my child, and the closest thing
to being cared for is to care for someone else.

JOHN

It was friendly of you to offer to give me a lift. But why did
you take me home with you?

MOLLIE

Maybe it was just instinct.

JOHN

Instinct?

MOLLIE

I was worried about money and suddenly it occurred to me
to take in a boarder.

JOHN

It occurred to you then and there.

MOLLIE

As soon as I saw you up close.

JOHN

Why did you pick me up?

MOLLIE

I liked your looks. Simple — just instinct.

JOHN

You gave me supper.

MOLLIE

Just vegetable soup — the second day, which is the best day —
and cornsticks. You ate three helpings.

JOHN

It was an evening of rising appetites. You showed me the
room and gave me a toothbrush and a pair of pajamas. Whose
toothbrush was it?

MOLLIE

Mine. I washed it thoroughly with soda.

JOHN

And the pajamas?

MOLLIE

Phillip's —

JOHN

It began to rain — you said it had set in for the night — and
your words, your voice, were somehow extraordinary.

MOLLIE

Everything was perfectly ordinary. I showed you the room
and mentioned the price with board. You said you'd take it.

JOHN

I was looking at you — not the room. Room and board in
Rockland County is the last thing in the world I needed. I

have a perfectly good apartment in New York, two blocks
from the office.

MOLLIE

An apartment in town? Why didn't you tell me?

JOHN

You didn't ask me. You just showed me the room and there
was some misunderstanding. I had anticipated something else.

MOLLIE

What did you anticipate?

JOHN

Mollie, when a woman picks up a stranger and takes him to
her room — the man naturally anticipates.

MOLLIE

You mean you thought it was something to do with — sex?

JOHN

I waited in the bed — I called two or three times.

MOLLIE

I was in the kitchen, going over grocery tickets and figuring
with a pencil and paper. I didn't want to gyp you.

JOHN

After a long time it began to dawn on me that the room
business was no new gimmick — no come-on — I waited and
waited — have you ever waited like that — expecting someone
who never came?

MOLLIE

I have. But that is love. How could you imagine I would

think about sex with a man I had just met? How could you think that of me? Mollie Henderson? Mollie Henderson Lovejoy?

JOHN

Is that the way you usually pick your boarders?

MOLLIE

I never had a boarder before. But when I saw you walking down that lonesome road, it seemed somehow inevitable.

JOHN

I left the house in a fury, found and fixed my car and said to myself: John Tucker, you're a sucker. I was never going back, of course.

MOLLIE

You mean you meant never to come back?

JOHN

No, ma'am.

MOLLIE

Oh, John! Then we would never have known each other. Besides, you had paid for the room.

JOHN

All morning I was furious. Then, that afternoon, God help me, I was remembering you, Mollie. I remembered your face, your voice, and the way somehow it was all extraordinary. I had forgotten about being a sucker and then, much to my surprise, I began to drive all the way back to Rockland County. And then this crazy time began.

MOLLIE

Why do you say it's crazy? It's perfectly ordinary.

JOHN
It wasn't ordinary. Something magical happened.

MOLLIE
Magical?

JOHN
I suddenly felt the color of the earth and sky.

MOLLIE
When I first saw you, you looked lost and puzzled.

JOHN
There was no back or front to my life.

MOLLIE
But you're an architect.

JOHN
No back or front or depth. No design or meaning.

MOLLIE
Oh John!

JOHN
No color, pulse or form. But finally I met and loved you. You knew I loved you.

MOLLIE
Although you never said it until tonight. I knew the way you looked at me. I knew that you wanted to hold my hand. I knew that you even wanted to kiss me.

JOHN
But you were so evasive — Always wanted to talk about

something intellectual. And Paris was always coming in the room.

MOLLIE

After Phillip I wanted something so otherwise.

JOHN

What?

MOLLIE

I wanted someone who didn't want me for my body.

JOHN

Yes —

MOLLIE

I wanted somebody who would love me for my mind — my soul.

JOHN

I love you for your body.

MOLLIE

You too!

JOHN

And for your wisdom of heart and for your soul. I love you, baby, period.

(*He tries to kiss her.*)

MOLLIE

I can't kiss you, John. For the first time in my life I have to think and be practical.

JOHN
A kiss won't prevent — being practical.

MOLLIE
To other people a kiss is light and sweet. To me a kiss is sweet as syrup. But it's not light. In fact it leads straight to the dark. To sin, in fact.

JOHN
How so?

MOLLIE
When I first saw Phillip — when I was fifteen, that afternoon of the Peach Festival, he kissed me. My first kiss. And — I don't want to shock you, John.

JOHN
You're not shocking me.

MOLLIE
We kissed and kissed again.

JOHN
Yes?

MOLLIE
And then we — it may sound crude and vulgar — but we slept together.

JOHN
I see.

MOLLIE
That same afternoon. In the woods near Society City. In a briar patch, in fact.

JOHN
Was it comfortable?

MOLLIE
We moved from the briar patch later on. Doesn't that shock you?

JOHN
No, but don't dwell on it so much.

MOLLIE
I cried and cried. I knew it would have killed my father if he had known. I cried and wept and bawled. At first Phillip didn't want to marry me.

JOHN
Not marry my fifteen-year-old peach queen?

MOLLIE
No. Next morning he just sat in the kitchen drinking whiskey and looking cross.

JOHN
But then you got married.

MOLLIE
At two o'clock the next afternoon. So you see how a kiss that is warm and sweet can lead to sin and sorrow.

JOHN
Tell me, Mollie. Are you still in love with Phillip?

MOLLIE
I don't want to be.

JOHN
But are you?

MOLLIE
A thing like this once happened to me in my childhood. There was an old woman who used to work in the Delight Drugstore, at home in Society City. And she put a spell on me.

JOHN
A spell?

MOLLIE
Yes. I knew that if she looked into my eyes, I would have to do whatever she willed me to do. Wasn't that awful?

JOHN
What did the old woman will you to do?

MOLLIE
Once my daddy told me not to go into the Delight Drugstore and not to eat ice cream. And I chanced to see the old lady and she looked into my eyes. And against my will I was drawn into the Delight Drugstore and I ate ice cream. Against my daddy's wishes and against my will.

JOHN
But maybe you wanted to eat ice cream.

MOLLIE
No. It was against my will. The first time with Phillip it was not against my will.

JOHN
And the second time, Mollie?

MOLLIE

I was under his spell. Love is very much like witches and
ghosts, and childhood. When it speaks to you, you have to
answer, and you have to go wherever it tells you to go.

JOHN

Do you still believe in witches and spells?

MOLLIE

I'm grown now, but sometimes —

JOHN

When I was a child, I went to a Chautauqua and there was a
man who hypnotized people. Old ladies rode bicycles on the
stage. A gentleman in spats, very dignified, stood on his head.
Everybody laughed. The whole tent rocked with laughter,
but I remember as a child, I was so horrified I was sick.

MOLLIE

Although I adore shows and circuses I don't like to watch
people make fools of themselves. Are you saying I'm making
a fool of myself about Phillip?

JOHN

Are you still in love with him?

MOLLIE

I fell in love with Phillip at first sight. At that time he was
engaged to the Governor's daughter. Mother Lovejoy said
Phillip flew high and lit low.

JOHN

Mother Lovejoy must be a prize old bitch to say that.

MOLLIE

That's what I always thought in the back of my mind. But after all, she was Phillip's only mother. Aristocrats. And she was heartsick about Sister.

JOHN

What had Sister done to make her heartsick?

MOLLIE

She came out fifteen years ago, and nothing ever happened. She never married. Works in the library, whispers — she breaks my heart. I love her. Most sisters-in-law don't love each other, but I do love Sister.

JOHN

Whispers?

MOLLIE

It's from working in the library. Even when she comes home, she whispers. Just reads and whispers, and writes in notebooks from time to time. She once fell in love with a man in Z.

JOHN

What do you mean — a man in Z?

MOLLIE

He was standing before the Z Section in the library.

JOHN

What was he doing in Z?

MOLLIE

Just taking out *Rats, Lice and History*, by somebody Zimmerman. I don't know what he was doing, but it was love at first sight.

JOHN

A whispering sister in the Z Section does not sound like the same family with Phillip Lovejoy.

MOLLIE

Sister is gentle — but Phillip — he struck me, he beat me up so many times. Once he tore off my nightgown and put me out of that front door . . .

(*Points to door.*)

naked as a jaybird. And I stood it!

JOHN

Why, Mollie?

MOLLIE

I — why we — I — In spite of all Phillip's terrible failings he had a lot of charm. A redeeming charm, somebody once said.

JOHN (*Ironically*)

I get it.

MOLLIE

I stood it. I stood the beatings-up. The time I was locked out of the house buck naked. I stood it all. Until he — did something I couldn't forgive.

JOHN

What on earth did Phillip do you couldn't forgive?

MOLLIE

He began hurting my feelings. He said I used clichés.

JOHN

Clichés?

MOLLIE

That's a French way of saying a person is next door to a fool.

JOHN

And that hurt more than the beatings?

MOLLIE

Far, far more. I had only brought him up a plate of spaghetti when he was working. And seeing him so tense and worried I said to him, just to comfort him, "Art is long and life is fleeting." Then he used that word and he dumped the plate of spaghetti all over the typewriter. That limp tomato spaghetti and that hard black typewriter.

JOHN

So you got a divorce on the grounds of a cliché?

MOLLIE

Not only that, John.

JOHN

For God's sake what else, Mollie?

MOLLIE

I realized, John, that Phillip was unfaithful to me, in fact, I realized he was polygamous.

JOHN

Dear me!

MOLLIE

I didn't want to realize it. It was like a cloud on a summer's day.

JOHN
What did you do?

MOLLIE
I tried to be a brass monkey.

JOHN
See no evil, hear no evil, speak no evil.

MOLLIE
Exactly. But after the clichés and spaghetti, polygamy was just too much. I had to get a divorce because of my pride and because of Paris' pride. I had custody of Paris, of course, and Phillip had good visiting privileges.

JOHN
Tell me, Mollie, why did you remarry Phillip Lovejoy?

MOLLIE
I — I was under a spell — a strange spell. When you've been married to a man and he is allowed by court injunction to visit his son . . .

JOHN
Did he come often?

MOLLIE
Yes. He got to coming frequently. At first he came on weekends. Then it was reversed.

JOHN
Reversed?

MOLLIE
The weekends were longer and longer. Soon he stayed all

the time and only went to New York on the weekends. So under the circumstances —

JOHN

Yes, it would be a shame to be living in sin with a man you've been married to once before.

MOLLIE

That's what I thought. But hindsight is wiser than foresight.

JOHN

That's what they say.

MOLLIE

It seems to me that Phillip was happy so many times, but never knew it. When he realized he was happy, then he was sad. Because then it was finished. Even after he wrote "The Chinaberry Tree" he was unhappy.

JOHN

That was his successful book.

MOLLIE

Yes. The only one. Sometimes I wish he had never written it. It gave him all the kudoes and a fortune, but it was such a great success he began to hate it. For years after he couldn't work.

JOHN

Didn't he write another book?

MOLLIE

Yes. And when that went badly, he blamed me, Paris, the city. Mother Lovejoy bought this apple farm for us. We were going to do manual labor.

JOHN

Who was going to do manual labor?

MOLLIE

All of us. But instead, Phillip started a play. He said it was easier. We all had such hopes. Then he got restless, and went to Mexico.

JOHN

To gather local color?

MOLLIE

Maybe so, but not for the play. He found somebody else and got a Mexican divorce. And for almost a year it was like somebody with a terrible chisel was cracking at my heart all day long and every night.

JOHN

What about his play?

MOLLIE

The play was set a hundred years from now after everybody had been destroyed by some moon-bomb. There were only two people left on earth; a man, a woman and a snake. You see, it was awfully symbolic.

JOHN

I see.

MOLLIE

Maybe that's why it failed. On opening night the audience started leaving during the first act. Mother Lovejoy stood in the lobby and tried to herd them back into their seats like a sheep dog.

JOHN
Where was that?

MOLLIE
In Boston, a month ago. Yankees are so cold. After the curtain fell, Phillip went back to the hotel and slashed his wrists. Writing plays must be a terrible shock to the nervous system.

JOHN
Particularly if they close on opening night.

MOLLIE
I don't think Phillip wanted to die. But Mother Lovejoy sent him to this sanatorium. He's there now. Poor Phillip.

JOHN
Have you ever kissed anyone else but Phillip?

MOLLIE
Why naturally not.

JOHN
No one?

MOLLIE
Of course not, outside the family. I told you, when I kiss, something very peculiar happens to me.

JOHN
It's not that peculiar.

MOLLIE
After a kiss my head is swirled and crazy. My legs turn to macaroni.

(*He kisses her.*)

Cooked macaroni.

(SISTER *appears, dressed in a robe and curlpapers.*)

JOHN
Look.

MOLLIE
Sister. Are you all right?

SISTER
I thought I heard voices. Am I disturbing you?

MOLLIE
Of course not. You look flustered and unnerved. What's the matter?

SISTER
The wind and the banging.

MOLLIE
It's that garage door that keeps banging whenever there is a wind.

SISTER
It scared me.

JOHN
I'll secure it.

(*He exits.*)

MOLLIE (*Calling after him*)
The tool kit is in the garage.

(*To Sister*)

Sister, you've been tense and troubled ever since you came this morning. What is it?

SISTER
I needed to talk to you alone. Without Mother or Paris around.

MOLLIE
A sisterly talk, darling? Or trouble?

SISTER
Both.

MOLLIE
Mother Lovejoy said Phillip is brown as a nut.

SISTER
Brown as a nut is all very well — but it's about Phillip I have to tell you. He's coming tomorrow.

MOLLIE
Tomorrow? Phillip coming?

SISTER
Phillip wants you, Mollie. He's going to ask you to marry him again.

MOLLIE
He's so erratic. Or is it erotic? I always confuse the two words.

SISTER
Erratic denotes going every which way. Eros is the god of love.

MOLLIE
Either word will do.

SISTER
Do you still love my brother?

MOLLIE
Phillip abandoned us. But when he comes in the door, when he looks into my eyes, and when he — I — I always know exactly what he wants.

SISTER
It's probably always the same thing.

MOLLIE
It's not me doing it. Me, Mollie Henderson.

SISTER
Phillip is a boy that sex throws right off his rocker.

MOLLIE
As I well know.

SISTER
He has led you a merry dance.

MOLLIE
It wasn't merry. I had a sad slice of life with him.

SISTER
Are you going to marry Phillip a third time?

MOLLIE

I don't want to.

SISTER

There's no law that requires you to keep marrying and marrying him.

MOLLIE

No law?

SISTER

No legal law, that is. And no prizes for marriage marathons.

MOLLIE

It's only that when I look into his eyes — his eyes are blue with yellow flecks. I can't describe it.

SISTER

I have observed it.

MOLLIE

You're so pure-minded. It's difficult . . .

SISTER

You would be surprised to know what goes on sometimes in my mind.

MOLLIE

Why? Have you ever loved a man, Sister?

SISTER

Yes.

MOLLIE

Oh, my precious. I'm so glad. Is he a Society City man?

SISTER

No.

MOLLIE

From Atlanta?

SISTER

Never Atlanta.

MOLLIE

Well, what? Where?

SISTER

My love lives in other countries — always far away.

MOLLIE

You mean a foreign man? What does Mother Lovejoy say?

SISTER

Mother doesn't know. And it's not one man, but many.

MOLLIE

Many foreigners? Oh, Sister, you are excited after your trip. Rest with me.

SISTER

My loves are not real to anybody else. But they are real to me.

MOLLIE

Oh, imaginary friends.

SISTER

There's one in particular that I've had a long time. His name is Angelo. We live in foreign places and we love each other like married people love. Does this shock you, Mollie?

MOLLIE

No, my darling.

SISTER

Another time I had a lover called Rocco, but he died of something terrible, and so did I, in a kind of lingering way. It went on night after night, like chapters. It was terrible but in that kind of daydream, it was fascinating too, because we loved each other so much. And when you love each other very much, death is romantic so long as you die together.

MOLLIE

Although your loves are only daydreams, they must be a comfort to you. Like John is a comfort to me.

SISTER

John? The man who is fixing the door? The tenant in the barn?

MOLLIE

John Tucker. Isn't that a lovely name? He's in love with me.

SISTER

Don't hurt him, Mollie.

MOLLIE

I'd cut off my ears, sew down my eyelids and pull out my tongue before I'd hurt him.

SISTER

Gracious, Mollie. You swear like a child.

MOLLIE

He's in love with me, and I couldn't hurt him.

(MOTHER LOVEJOY *enters from upstairs, dressed like Sister in robe and curlpapers.*)

MOTHER LOVEJOY
Mollie, is there any milk of magnesia or castoria?

MOLLIE
I'll get it. It's on the shelf in the kitchen.

(*She exits.*)

MOTHER LOVEJOY
Travel is so binding. And that northern train food. I heard talking when I woke up. And nothing aggravates me more than knowing that somebody is saying something in a house that I don't hear. I am only happy when I'm in the center of things.

SISTER
Well, here you are.

MOLLIE (*Re-entering*)
Sister told me Phillip is coming tomorrow.

MOTHER LOVEJOY
Loreena Lovejoy, you know I always like to be the one to tell important news.

MOLLIE
But is Phillip ready to leave the sanatorium?

MOTHER LOVEJOY
He's dying to get out.

MOLLIE

But is he ready?

MOTHER LOVEJOY

Phillip needs you, Mollie, and wants to marry you again.

MOLLIE

I didn't think you liked Phillip being married to me.

MOTHER LOVEJOY

The first time I nearly had a stroke. The second time I was bitter but resigned. But now I am used to it. Economics and common sense.

MOLLIE

Economics?

MOTHER LOVEJOY

That sanatorium, dear girl, costs one thousand six hundred dollars a month.

SISTER

But you have all that money that Uncle Willie left you.

MOTHER LOVEJOY

Yes, a beautiful will. Such a fair will. I was only a cousin twice removed, but I was the chief beneficiary. Such a fair will and such a surprise to everybody. It's a case of still waters run deep.

SISTER

Not that Uncle Willie was ever still.

MOTHER LOVEJOY

He had locomotor ataxia. An old-fashioned disease that hap-

pens sometimes to aristocrats. But nobody connected with
stocks, oil wells, business ventures. In fact, he was supposed
to be a little irresponsible, bless his heart. He came to me in
a mysterious way too.

MOLLIE
Mysterious?

MOTHER LOVEJOY
Toward evening, just before supper, when there was the
smell of turnip greens, Uncle Willie walked up the front
porch and sat down in the rocking chair. He said, "Ophelia,
I've come to this house and I've come to stay." Rocking,
smelling, listening, "I've come to this house and I've come
to stay." Mysterious, really. Then he said something kind of
cute. "Aside from the greens, what else is there for supper?"

MOLLIE
Weren't you surprised?

MOTHER LOVEJOY
Well, frankly, at first I was *appalled*. But he stayed on with
us eleven years, eating buttermilk ice cream every day with
a napkin round his chin, and oiling my sewing machine and
raking the yard.

MOLLIE
How much money did Uncle Willie leave you?

MOTHER LOVEJOY
Don't you know, Mollie, that you can ask poor people about
their finances, but it's not tactful to ask the well-to-do? Law,
children, do you know what time it is?

MOLLIE
Yes, it is late.

MOTHER LOVEJOY

You people in the North stay up like people in Russian plays.
Come on, Sister.

(*As she exits, whispering*)

Did your bowels move?

(JOHN *returns*.)

JOHN

Phillip's mother doesn't stay very long, does she?

MOLLIE

No. But Phillip stays longer and it makes me nervous.

JOHN

Why does it make you nervous?

MOLLIE

When you loved a man and you're divorced, it just makes you
nervous.

JOHN

Is Phillip coming again?

MOLLIE

Yes.

JOHN

When?

MOLLIE

Tomorrow.

JOHN
What are you going to do?

MOLLIE
I've already broken the Ten Commandments with him.

JOHN
All ten?

MOLLIE
Not all ten of them.

JOHN
Hast thou made any graven images?

MOLLIE
Of course not.

JOHN
Coveted thy neighbor's ox or ass?

MOLLIE
My neighbor's ass?

JOHN
We'll check that one off.

MOLLIE
The everyday one.

JOHN
Oh, that one.

MOLLIE
But it wasn't me doing it. Me! Mollie Henderson! Reared

in the first Baptist Church of Society City. I got five gold stars for attendance.

JOHN
You slept with him, Mollie, after the divorce.

MOLLIE
I know it was a sin. But it's not adultery. Two times I said, "I, Mollie, take thee, Phillip, to be my lawful husband. To have and to hold. For richer or poorer. For better or worse. In sickness and in health."

JOHN
Hush, Mollie!

MOLLIE
"Till death us do part." Two times I said it to a preacher. How could it be adultery.

(*She knocks on wood.*)

JOHN
What are you doing?

MOLLIE
Knocking on wood.

JOHN
Why do you do that?

MOLLIE
I don't want it to happen again. But somehow three bad things go together.

JOHN
Like what?

MOLLIE
Three blind mice. Three witches.

JOHN
And going down three times when you drown.

MOLLIE
Sometimes I feel that Phillip and I are like two magnets running together.

JOHN
Mollie, have you ever thought of marrying me?

MOLLIE
You never asked me.

JOHN
I'm asking you now.

MOLLIE
Have you ever been in love before?

JOHN
Of course. Lots of times.

MOLLIE
But you never married.

JOHN
I did.

MOLLIE

What was she like — your wife?

JOHN

Very beautiful. It's hard to describe. Hard to remember. I loved her.

MOLLIE

What happened?

JOHN

It was just as I was finished with the Navy. I was doing construction work — really just a laborer — we were very happy or so it seemed to me. Then my wife fell in love with another man, although she said she loved me too.

MOLLIE

What a predicament.

JOHN

Then still another man. It came to the point when I went in the front door I would feel someone going out the back door.

MOLLIE

That's unbelievable.

JOHN

Though I loved her so very much, I had to leave.

MOLLIE

And you still loved her.

JOHN

Still I loved her but I had to leave. Before I met my wife I was a four-by-four person and then I was cut down to a three-by-four. Before I was cut down to a two-by-four man I divorced her and used the GI bill to study. I always wanted to be an architect.

MOLLIE

I don't see how anybody could treat you like that, John. She must have been crazy, or something.

JOHN

Call it sick, Mollie. But I was so much in love with her. We had a cottage on the beach and I used to cook shore dinners.

MOLLIE

A *shore* dinner?

JOHN

You dig a pit in the sand, light a fire and let it burn to coals. You have lobster, clams, and layers of seaweed in between, then more lobster, more clams. You can make it as complicated as you want, with ears of roasted corn or potatoes. The shore dinner bakes for a whole afternoon in the hot sand. Then, at evening, when the sky is darkening and the waves dark and shushing on the shore, you dig into the shore dinner. I have not made a shore dinner since then or watched the flickering twilight on the ocean since that time.

MOLLIE

And yet she was unfaithful to you. Women can talk on and on about sorrow, but when a man grieves, he doesn't say a word. When my father lost the hardware and notion store, he sat at home and never said a word — bankrupt — the store taken away from him. He grieved to death and never said a word. Nobody could help him.

JOHN

I sometimes thought of love again, but you can't plan love, it's something that comes round cornerwise when you least expect it.

MOLLIE

Like the day we met on Danger Road.

JOHN

And the color and pulse of life returned.

MOLLIE

Do you believe in God?

JOHN

Tonight I believe in Him altogether.

MOLLIE

But God is nothing you can see.

JOHN

Love is nothing you can see either. But like God, it is everywhere. It's not like the chair, the clock, the table. You don't see it, you see through it.

MOLLIE

Straight through it?

JOHN

Love is transparent. When you're in love there's a light in your eyes and that light makes the chair, the clock, the table look luminous.

MOLLIE

Luminous? Like your watch dial is luminous?

JOHN

Luminous as love is luminous. Marry me, Mollie, marry me soon.

MOLLIE

Would it be a cliché, John, if I said that love is so all of a sudden, and that I want to sleep on it, in the back of my mind?

JOHN

I'll be right across in the barn. In the meantime, good night, love.

MOLLIE

Nighty-night.

(JOHN *exits.* MOLLIE *goes in a daze, touches the table, touches the chair, starts to wind the clock. We notice* PHILLIP LOVEJOY *for the first time, standing at the foot of the stairs. He is holding a small bouquet of flowers.*)

MOLLIE

Phillip, where did you come from?

PHILLIP

Where do I come from?
Where do I go?
Where do I come from?
My cotton-eyed Joe.

MOLLIE

How you startled me.

PHILLIP

I walked from the station.

MOLLIE

All that way.

PHILLIP

Saw a light at the window and you here with a man.

MOLLIE

John Tucker, an architect.

PHILLIP

I went up the back stairs.

MOLLIE

Why?

PHILLIP

I wanted to see you alone. Look, Mollie, everything's the same. The same chair, table. Same furniture. The same rug. It seems so long ago. And there's the clock.

MOLLIE

The grandfather clock. It puts me in mind of peace and family.

PHILLIP

It puts me in mind of time. You were winding it when I came back. Busily, busily winding time. I hate clocks.

MOLLIE

It has a lovely chime.

PHILLIP

What's the matter, Mollie? You look so strange.

MOLLIE
Nothing.

PHILLIP
Are you afraid of me, Mollie?

MOLLIE
I am proud of you, Phillip. Proud of the way you faced up to the sanatorium.

PHILLIP
I didn't face up to it.

MOLLIE
What was it like at Blythe View?

PHILLIP
It was like nothingness and nothingness is horrible, for nothingness is death.

MOLLIE
Should I wake up Paris, Mother Lovejoy and Sister?

PHILLIP
No, I want to see you alone. I have got to talk to you.

MOLLIE
What about?

PHILLIP
What I was and what I am now.

MOLLIE
It's late, Phillip. It is almost dawn.

PHILLIP

I see the dawn, the colors crushed and cold on the horizon. Strips of lemon peel and orange. I see the dawn and I can describe it, but I can't feel it. I can describe so many things. Like food — homemade blueberry cobblers, the dumplings and the golden lattice crust. But I can't taste it.

MOLLIE

I'll make some for you tomorrow.

PHILLIP

And flowers, Mollie. The tulips, jonquils and lilacs. I can describe them all against this watery light. But I no longer feel the joy of them. And love I can describe too, but I can't feel it.

MOLLIE

Why did you come back, Phillip?

PHILLIP

I want to feel again. And taste and smell. I want to live again.

MOLLIE

It's always so sudden when I see you after a long time.

PHILLIP

What's sudden?

MOLLIE

Just you — the look of you. But now I have to be adult and practical.

PHILLIP

Why on earth, baby?

MOLLIE
Because ten days ago I rented the barn apartment.

PHILLIP
You mean that guy you were here with?

MOLLIE
Yes, he's my support — my moral support.

PHILLIP
What does he have to do with us? What does anybody have
to do with us?

MOLLIE
We're not the only people in the world, Phillip.

PHILLIP
Between the rest of the world and us there's always been a
curtain — like a Pullman curtain. Don't you remember that?
Don't you remember me and you in the nighttime? In the
daytime, too.

MOLLIE
Naturally. It happened.

PHILLIP
I'll tell you a secret, Mollie.

MOLLIE
What?

PHILLIP
I'm not through.

MOLLIE

Is that the secret?

PHILLIP

I am going to write the greatest goddam novel of this genera-
tion. And I'll write it upstairs. Here on the farm. And the
work, the world, the wonder will begin again.

MOLLIE

But —

PHILLIP

I feel the wonder rising as the wind is rising in the night.
After the black dark years I feel it rising. You have to love
me.

MOLLIE

Do you still love me, Phillip?

PHILLIP

Love you?

(*Shakes head negatively.*)

I feel surrounded by a zone of loneliness. I try to reach out
and touch, but I can only grab. For the thing only is
immortal.

(*He touches table, chair.*)

This table, this chair. These things will live beyond me.

MOLLIE

If you don't love me, why did you come back?

PHILLIP

Like the sick person watches the well.
Like the dying watches the living.
No, Mollie, it's not love.

MOLLIE

Then what is it?

PHILLIP

Without you I am so exposed, I am skinless. From the beginning you knew I had to live in a cocoon. You knew I had
to live with you and be protected. It is not my fault, it is
just an act of nature.

MOLLIE

But cocoons are dead.

PHILLIP

Yes. Cocoons are dead.

MOLLIE

I don't want to die, Phillip.

PHILLIP

Listen Mollie, just listen.

How shall I guard my soul so that it be
Touched not by thine? And shall it be brought,
    Lifted above thee, unto other things?

    Ah gladly would I hide it utterly
Lost in the dark where are no murmurings,
    In strange and silent places that do not
Vibrate when the deep soul quivers and sings.

But all that touches us two makes us twin,
Even as the bow crossing the violin
Draws but one voice from the two strings that meet.
Upon what instrument are we two spanned?

And what great player has us in his hand?
O song most sweet.

MOLLIE
It's so beautiful, Phillip.

PHILLIP
Yes, it's beautiful, but I didn't write it. Come on up to bed.

MOLLIE
I'd better put these flowers in some water.

PHILLIP
Hurry on up.

(*Starts upstairs.*)

MOLLIE (*To herself*)
These flowers need an aspirin.

(PHILLIP *goes upstairs.* MOLLIE *opens Paris' door, turns off lights, stands for a moment, then* PARIS *enters.*)

MOLLIE
Paris?

PARIS
What's the matter, Mother? Why aren't you asleep?

MOLLIE

My child, if your mother told you she is in love with two people, what would you think?

PARIS

Love. To me love is funny. Funny peculiar and funny ha-ha.

MOLLIE

Did you say your prayers?

PARIS

Yes, Mother.

MOLLIE

What did you pray?

PARIS

Do I have to tell you?

MOLLIE

No, Lambie. I'm not nosey or anything like that — but a mother . . .

PARIS

To hell you're not nosey.

MOLLIE

But being in love with two people — what would you do, Lambie?

PARIS

I don't know. It makes me sad when you talk so serious and growny.

MOLLIE
John said love is luminous. Let's see.

PARIS
How?

MOLLIE
Look at the table and think about someone you love. Close
your eyes.

> (*She closes her eyes. By now light of the dawn is
> coming through the window.*)

Phillip Ralston Lovejoy.

> (*Opens her eyes slowly.*)

Oh God, the table is shining.

PARIS
It's a plain wooden table —

MOLLIE (*Looks hard at chair, and closes eyes.*)

John Tucker.

> (*Opens eyes.*)

The chair is luminous. Both! How can you, table? How can
you, chair?

PARIS
It's a plain wooden chair.

> (*Exits.*)

PHILLIP

Mollie!

(She goes to the front door, looks up the stairs.)

Mollie!

(She touches the table, then the chair as . . .)

THE CURTAIN FALLS

ACT II

Time: The next afternoon.

At Rise: There is no one on stage. There is the sound of a typewriter. HATTIE BROWN and PARIS enter through kitchen door. Hattie is a buxom girl a year older than Paris.

HATTIE

That examination was a real brain-cracker. Describe the aims of Thomas Jefferson. Who was the originator of the Monroe Doctrine?

PARIS

The Monroe Doctrine reminds me of Marilyn Monroe and when I think about her I can't keep my mind on a test. That's the hardest part. Keeping your mind on a test.

HATTIE

All during that test there was this fly. All I could think about was this fly buzzing against the window, when I had so many other things to think about. Ordinarily I never notice flies. Who's writing on the typewriter?

PARIS

Daddy.

HATTIE (*Fearfully*)

Is *he* here?

PARIS

He came last night.

HATTIE

I've got to go.

PARIS

Don't go.

HATTIE

I've got to go. My great-aunt Jane was in an institution, but she was only a great-step-aunt.

PARIS

What's that got to do with the price of eggs?

HATTIE

Sonny Jenkins says your father is crazy.

PARIS

That runty screwball. I beat him up.

HATTIE

I heard he beat you.

PARIS

After he wrote his play Daddy rested in a rest home. Anything wrong with that?

HATTIE

We all read in the *Daily News* about what he did.

PARIS

Daddy's name has been in the papers many times — ever since I was born.

HATTIE

I know he's famous but —

PARIS

Daddy rested in the rest home for a few months and now he's well. The rest home was nice, lots of tennis playing and tea served in the afternoon.

HATTIE

I thought places like that were creepy.

PARIS

Tennis and drinking tea in the afternoon?

HATTIE

I didn't know they served afternoon tea to crazy people.

PARIS

Don't say crazy. Mother said, say sick. Daddy was not even sick.

HATTIE

I've got to go.

PARIS

Why? You just came.

HATTIE

I'm afraid of your father. Besides Mother told me never to come here, Paris.

PARIS

Why?

HATTIE

On account of we took off our clothes and looked at each other.

PARIS
Why did you tell her?

HATTIE
I always tell Mother everything. Don't you?

PARIS
No. Besides she wouldn't have minded.

HATTIE
Not mind it? Mother was deeply shocked.

(*She likes the word.*)

— deeply shocked.

(*She puts her arms around Paris.*)

— but Paris, I'm crazy about you — excuse me. I shouldn't have used that word. I mean I'm mad about you.

(PHILLIP *enters.*)

PHILLIP
Forever wilt thou love and she be fair.

HATTIE (*In confusion*)
I've got to go —

(*Exits running.*)

PHILLIP
Fair Helen —

PARIS
Her name is Hattie.

PHILLIP
Did I come in at the end or the beginning?

PARIS
I don't know what you mean.

PHILLIP
A boy of fourteen should.

PARIS
I'm not fourteen.

PHILLIP
How old are you?

PARIS
Going on thirteen. Last year you sent me a little midget space suit for my birthday. Why don't you remember my age?

PHILLIP
I try to.

PARIS
A little midget space suit. The truth is, Daddy, I can never really count on you as far as presents go.

PHILLIP
I have another present for you, Son.

(*Goes to cupboard, brings out chess set.*)

PARIS
What is it?

PHILLIP
This chess set.

PARIS
But it is yours. Your father made it.

PHILLIP
Yes, he carved it.

PARIS
He was a master artist when he carved.

PHILLIP
The chess set reminds me of home.

PARIS
Which home?

PHILLIP
When we bought this farm, to me, it was like buying Walden.

PARIS
Walden?

PHILLIP
Thoreau's home. I dreamed about home and I saw myself.

PARIS
This place?

PHILLIP
I was going to stop drinking and buy a cow.

PARIS
But you hate milk, Daddy.

PHILLIP
For the better portion of my life I have yearned to like milk better than whiskey, but I never could.

PARIS
Too bad.

PHILLIP
I saw myself getting up at dawn — milking the cow —

PARIS
But you never bought the cow.

PHILLIP
But I saw myself. I saw myself working in the garden —

PARIS
You know good and well you paid me to take care of the garden, Daddy.

PHILLIP
And tending the green curled lettuce, the dusty summer corn, the eggplant and purple cabbages.

PARIS
You paid me two dollars a week.

PHILLIP
And then came breakfast, pancakes and sausages of home-raised pork.

PARIS
You only drink black coffee for breakfast.

PHILLIP

But I saw myself. I saw myself working on my novel every morning. Then in the afternoon there were fences to be mended, wood to be split.

PARIS

You can still do that. This place is in a shambles.

PHILLIP

I saw the farm in all its weathers — the mild, sweet days of May — and the green summer pond. The blue October and the apples.

PARIS

You worked the still, Daddy, and made applejack.

PHILLIP

Yeah, I did that. I saw the snowbound spells and I saw myself finishing a whole short novel at one stretch. Did you ever read "The Turn of the Screw," Son?

PARIS

Did you write it, Daddy?

PHILLIP

No. But I wish I had.

PARIS

Don't look so sad, Daddy.

PHILLIP

A funny thing, Paris.

PARIS

What's funny?

PHILLIP

I thought that once I got back to the apple farm I would write like a house afire. But all morning long I've been sitting on my can just writing snips and snatches. Snips and snatches. I think I'll go upstairs and put my nose back to the grindstone.

MOLLIE (*Offstage*)
Lambie, Lambie!

(PHILLIP *exits upstairs.* MOLLIE *enters with two bags of groceries.*)

PARIS
Why are you crying, Mother?

MOLLIE
Am I crying?

PARIS
There are tears in your eyes.

MOLLIE
Lambie, come and help me. The cost of celery is out of this world these days.

PARIS
I could do without celery for ever.

MOLLIE
But you have to have a well-balanced diet. Celery for the blood, carrots for the eyes and spinach for the iron. What are you eating, Paris?

PARIS
Pickles and cake.

MOLLIE

Pickles and cake? It's combinations like that that give you that awful gas.

PARIS

I wish you wouldn't say things like that. It embarrasses me.

MOLLIE

But it's true, Lambie . . .

> (PARIS *exits, slamming door behind him.* MOTHER LOVEJOY *enters, followed by* SISTER, *who takes a book down from shelf and starts to read.*)

MOLLIE

It's terrible when a child slams a door in his mother's face. Even to shut it is bad enough. How sharper than a serpent's tooth it is to have a thankless child. That's Shakespeare. Required reading my last year of school.

SISTER

How old were you when you quit school, Mollie?

MOLLIE

Fourteen years old. I had read every bit of *King Lear* and was in the first grade of Spanish — *cierra la puerta* — do you speak Spanish, Mother Lovejoy?

MOTHER LOVEJOY

No. We had French at the Peachtree Female Academy. *Parlez-vous français?*

MOLLIE

No. It's curious that with all the long years of schooling I had, the only thing that stuck to me was that part about the

serpent's tooth and *cierra la puerta*. It means "shut the door"
in Spanish.

MOTHER LOVEJOY
A curious thing to stick with you.

SISTER
You learned more than a serpent's tooth, Mollie.

MOTHER LOVEJOY
All night long I had my thinking cap on. Thinking, remembering, worrying. Do you remember, Mollie, how you looked
the last time we were here?

MOLLIE
Just before Phillip left?

MOTHER LOVEJOY
You had fallen off so I was afraid you were going into a
decline. I commented to myself — at last Mollie's lost her
looks.

MOLLIE
You didn't comment it to yourself. You commented it to me.

MOTHER LOVEJOY
But now you're just as you used to be before Phillip left you.
That old figure — the old color — the old life in your eyes.

SISTER
Mollie never looked more beautiful — radiant, in fact.

MOTHER LOVEJOY
I say to myself, what is it? Is it vitamins, vitality? No, I am
forced to conclude. I've given Sister vitamins since childhood

— vitamins, cod liver oil, liver, spinach. Thin as she is, she eats like a field hand, but what does it do for her?

SISTER

I'm healthy. That's what it does for me.

MOTHER LOVEJOY

Since it's not vitamins. Not vitality. I've come to the conclusion just what the one thing is.

SISTER

What are you talking about?

MOTHER LOVEJOY

It's a word I have never used before — no lady should ever use. But I'm glad it's out in the open.

SISTER

What's out in the open?

MOTHER LOVEJOY

S–E–X, that's what's out in the open.

SISTER

Is that why you had on your thinking cap last night?

MOTHER LOVEJOY

Look at you. When you hold up your shoulders you're more graceful than Mollie. Your form is — more to my taste than Mollie's. I like a fragile, aristocratic form. Your voice is well-bred, musical. You are a lady to the manor born.

MOLLIE

And Sister is intellectual —

MOTHER LOVEJOY

But what does it all fetch her? Without that three-letter word. Daintiness, charm, breeding avails us nothing. For that three-letter word makes the world go round.

SISTER

Am I going out of my mind?

MOTHER LOVEJOY

No! But you're much too high-minded or dense to understand. S–E–X. Why must you flout me so?

SISTER

How do I flout you?

MOTHER LOVEJOY

When you were eighteen you came out at the Peachtree Cotillion. Best prepared debut of any girl in Georgia. White ball dress with a million teensy little tucks. I made it myself. When we went to the Cotillion, I had visions of princes and would-be presidents — I had such visions. And what happened?

SISTER

I vomited.

MOTHER LOVEJOY

After all my hopes and dreams, she stood on the ballroom floor and there — right there —

SISTER

I couldn't help it, Mother, it was just excitement.

MOTHER LOVEJOY

That's how you flout me, miss. In my day a girl didn't have

to depend on that three-letter word. Those were the days when charm, beauty and vivaciousness were appreciated. Just simple allure was enough. Gentlemen came from as far as Chattahoochee County and Joplin to court me. I was sought after, admired, proposed to, feted. I was the belle of Society City.

SISTER
Then you met Father.

MOTHER LOVEJOY
On a blazing afternoon I was crossing the courthouse square, then what did I see?

MOLLIE
Mr. Lovejoy?

MOTHER LOVEJOY
A Greek god who was a total stranger. Although the afternoon was blazing hot, I was chilled from the top of my scalp to the soles of my feet.

MOLLIE
You mean it was love at first sight?

SISTER
Sex — I think it was —

MOTHER LOVEJOY
Don't use that word.

SISTER
And then the catastrophe came.

MOTHER LOVEJOY
We won't go into that.

SISTER
He left you, Mother. He abandoned you with no funds and two children.

MOTHER LOVEJOY
Stop, Loreena.

SISTER
You tried every way to find him. You practically advertised.

MOTHER LOVEJOY
My family made discreet inquiries.

SISTER
But not a clue. Vanished he did and humiliated you as you try to humiliate me.

MOTHER LOVEJOY
Oh, there is that good-looking Mr. Tucker coming from the barn. I'd always set my cap for Sister to marry a doctor. Not that she is sick, but sometimes I'm ailing.

SISTER
What are you talking about?

MOTHER LOVEJOY
That watermelon-pink dress washes you out so.

SISTER
I'm going back upstairs.

MOTHER LOVEJOY
You stay right here and be vivacious.

(JOHN *enters.*)

Speak of the devil! Mr. Tucker, we were just talking about you.

JOHN
What were you saying?

MOTHER LOVEJOY
Are you a single man?

MOLLIE
Yes, divorced.

MOTHER LOVEJOY
Are you a professional man?

JOHN
I'm an architect.

MOTHER LOVEJOY
Then you are professional. Come sit over here on the couch by Sister. Hold up your shoulders, Sister. Don't poke your neck out like a turtle. Take off your glasses.

SISTER
I can't see without my glasses.

MOTHER LOVEJOY
When you were twelve, and I had to take you to the oculist, I whispered the letters to you. A belle with glasses is a lifetime ruined.

SISTER
She did, too. Did you ever hear of such a thing?

MOTHER LOVEJOY
But would you see the letters? Would you hear my whispers?

SISTER
The oculist heard you first and sent you out of the room.

MOTHER LOVEJOY
I'll go up and leave them to themselves tactfully. I'll go upstairs and cross-stitch. And Mollie, you go in the kitchen.

(MOTHER LOVEJOY *exits, as does* MOLLIE.)

SISTER
When things are arranged so obviously, it makes you feel flat, doesn't it? No matter what I would do, it would be flat. My feet feel flat, my head feels flat, and I really can't see without my glasses. I'm glad Mollie has you.

JOHN
I'm glad I have Mollie.

SISTER
How do people meet each other?

JOHN
They just meet.

SISTER
I mean as male and female who fall in love.

JOHN
I knew what you meant.

SISTER

But how?

JOHN

I met Mollie on an empty road. My car had broken down.

SISTER

Suppose your car hadn't broken down?

JOHN

I would have met Mollie somewhere else.

SISTER

My best friend Alice met her intended on a street corner while they were waiting for a bus.

JOHN

That's one way it could happen.

SISTER

Must I tramp on empty roads and wait for buses all my life? I am thirty-six years old. I can't even make small talk.

JOHN

Small talk?

SISTER

Like the weather and a man's hobbies. Unless a girl knows how to make small talk nothing big really happens to her.

JOHN

Who told you that?

SISTER

Mother. And nothing big has happened. For years I have

prayed to meet the right man, in the right place, at the right time, in the right dress. I have even gone to a fortuneteller.

JOHN

When I was a young man I went to a fortuneteller and she told me something awful.

SISTER

What did your fortune say?

JOHN

I was told for a long time, a very long time, I would only fall in love at first sight. And so I did. I fell in love at first sight a dozen times, and out of love as often.

SISTER

What a predicament!

JOHN

When I was in the Navy, I fell in love a hundred times. But nothing lasted, nothing stayed. It was only love at first sight.

SISTER

Love at first sight is terrible.

JOHN

Yes. I know.

SISTER

Like in *Romeo and Juliet*. Murder, tombs, poison and death everywhere.

JOHN

And practically no sex at all.

SISTER
But what other love is there?

JOHN
The gypsy said for many years I would only fall in love at
first sight and that was so. Then she said I would fall in
love at second sight, a hundred sight, a thousand sight. Right
down the line. And that too was so.

SISTER
What did you do, John?

JOHN
I married the girl.

(*He pauses.*)

Then the gypsy said I would lose my love and I would have
to start all over again.

SISTER
Fortunetelling and table-turning give me the creeps. But I
don't let them scare me. The first thing I say is "Don't tell
me anything bad. If you see trouble, don't tell me. Tell
me only the good things." That usually shuts them up. And
truthfully, I'm forty years old.

(MOLLIE *enters.*)

JOHN
I'm glad to have you as a friend, Loreena.

SISTER
Strange, we're friendly already! It seldom happens to me in
real life.

(*Hits her arm against banister.*)

Ouch!

MOLLIE

What's happened?

SISTER

I hit my funny bone. I wonder why they call it a funny bone when it hurts so much.

(SISTER *exits upstairs.*)

MOLLIE

What were you talking about?

JOHN

The logic of love.

MOLLIE

But love isn't logical. Suppose I hadn't been on that empty road, that day, that hour?

JOHN

We would have met somewhere else.

MOLLIE

Where?

JOHN

In the hand of the Statue of Liberty.

MOLLIE

There?

JOHN

It's logical.

MOLLIE

But —

JOHN

Or in the Panama Canal.

MOLLIE

Way down there?

JOHN

That too is logical.

MOLLIE

Seriously, what is this logic?

JOHN

I am serious. The longer I know you, Mollie, the more I am aware of that zany, crazy logic of love.

MOLLIE

There's something I want to tell you, John.

JOHN

What's that?

MOLLIE

I'm trying to tell you but I can't.

(*She turns away.*)

Anyway Phillip is home.

JOHN
You don't look very happy.

MOLLIE
I'm not.

(PARIS *enters with a lot of blueprints.*)

PARIS
What are these, John?

JOHN
Architect plans.

PARIS
What are they for?

JOHN
It's a house I'm going to build. A home.

MOLLIE (*Distracted*)
Where is it going to be?

JOHN
You'll decide. I want your help.

PARIS
Mother doesn't know doodley-squat about building houses.

JOHN
I think of it as a house on a hill that overlooks the river.
It's a strong house, made from native stone. And the north
wind, the east wind can howl and ricochet around the hill
and the house will stand.

MOLLIE
That sounds lovely, John.

JOHN
The walls are almost entirely of glass so that the sunlight shafts through the rooms and there is a sense of sparkle and light everywhere. The floors are flagstones with hot water pipes running underneath.

MOLLIE
Doesn't it burn your feet?

JOHN
No, Mollie, the flagstones are thick — and since the walls are glass we have to have a lot of trees and shrubs around for privacy.

MOLLIE
Still, I imagine you can't run around naked and you can't throw stones.

JOHN
And the kitchen . . .

MOLLIE
Oh, that reminds me. I've got to tend to dinner.

(*She exits.*)

JOHN
The boy's room is something super. There's a special closet for fishing rods and athletic equipment and even a bar . . .

PARIS
A bar?

JOHN

Where you can chin yourself.

PARIS

Oh.

JOHN

Just wait till I describe the boy's private bathroom. It's beautiful, practical and just opposite the can there's a TV set.

PARIS

That's practical. A boy always wants a private bathroom. Is the house going to be in Rockland County?

JOHN

I don't know. Don't you like Rockland County?

PARIS

I did — but something happened.

JOHN

What happened?

PARIS

My name — Paris.

JOHN

I don't quite get it.

PARIS

There was this little runty screwball, Sonny Jenkins. He started singing, "Paris is a crazy name and Paris' father's crazy." I fixed his clock for him all right.

JOHN

Attaboy.

PARIS

I broke his nose for him, and then when he was staggering, I punched his eyes. When both eyes were hanging out of his head on his cheeks, I stopped. You have seen that sort of thing, John.

JOHN

Yes. But it's rare.

PARIS

Then his gang took it up and sang "Paris is a crazy name, Paris' father's crazy." When everybody sings a thing enough, it begins to sound true, like television commercials. When the boys sang that my head began to swim and I cried — you understand, John, in front of everybody I cried — in public. This is what really happened, John. I couldn't even fight. I cried.

MOLLIE (*Entering from kitchen*)

I would never have believed it of Sonny Jenkins. If I had been there, I would have shook him until his teeth rattled.

PARIS

Oh, Mother, you were eavesdropping.

JOHN

Leave us alone, Mollie.

MOLLIE

I am a woman who has lived and suffered.

PARIS

There's just no privacy.

MOLLIE

Your mother is not shocked by anything. I, too, have cried in public.

PARIS

Mother, you eavesdrop and read diaries. I don't respect anybody who reads diaries. Sly people.

MOLLIE

I'm not sly. I just wanted to know what you were thinking.

(*She exits into kitchen.*)

PARIS

John, were your feelings ever hurt?

JOHN

Yes, I was about your age the year I had that awful acne. I was in love with this girl — very beautiful. But I idealized her so much I didn't dare to kiss her. You know when you idealize a girl that much, you are very careful about her self-respect.

PARIS (*With world-wise air*)

I know.

JOHN

Then one night we were sitting in the rumble seat of this car belonging to a pal of mine. He and his girl were smooching in the front seat and kissing, necking, and so forth. My pal wasn't a bit worried about *his* girl's self-respect. My girl and I were just pumping up a conversation about the moonlight and then suddenly I touched her face. I just stroked her face with my forefinger. Her skin was as soft as a flower petal. And then I *wanted* so much I couldn't stand it.

PARIS
What did you do, John?

JOHN
I put my arms around her and kissed her. I wanted it to go on for ever — but it only lasted a second. She pushed me away and said, "They say your face is not catching — but I'm afraid I might catch those bumps."

PARIS
She shouldn't have said that!

JOHN
And I had to sit there in that rumble seat — until my friends stopped smooching and the moonlight was very bright.

PARIS
Did you cry in public?

JOHN
I waited until I got home.

(Pause)

PARIS (Wants to comfort John)
You don't have a bit of acne now. Your skin is smooth as smooth. I wish I had as heavy a beard as that.

(Pause)

JOHN
I've worked up my own theory about matters like this.

PARIS
What's your theory about?

JOHN

The square root of sin.

PARIS

The what?

JOHN

The sin of hurting people's feelings. Of humiliating a person. That is the square root of sin. It's the same as murder.

PARIS

The same as murder?

JOHN

The square root is there. You just have to figure it to be a higher power. War is the square root of humiliation raised to the millionth power —

PARIS

To the millionth power?

JOHN

When you humiliate a person, it *is* a kind of murder. You are murdering his pride.

PARIS

I do like man-to-man talks.

JOHN

So do I.

PARIS

They're better than heart-to-heart. Heart-to-heart talks embarrass me.

(MOLLIE *enters from kitchen.*)

MOLLIE
Dinner is almost ready. Paris, if you look at your hands you'll admit they're potty.

PARIS
They've been pottier.

MOLLIE
That's not the point. Go wash them before dinner.

PARIS
Potty is such a potty word. I wish you wouldn't use it, Mother.

(*He exits.*)

MOLLIE
It's a perfectly good Anglo-Saxon word.

(PHILLIP *enters.*)

PHILLIP
Potty is as potty does. You must be the tenant in the barn.

MOLLIE
John Tucker — Phillip Lovejoy. John — Phillip.

PHILLIP
You were here a long time last night.

JOHN
And many nights before.

PHILLIP

That barn is where I work.

JOHN

What work?

PHILLIP

It's where I sit on my can. And it's my barn and my can. My quadge in fact.

JOHN

Your what?

PHILLIP

When I was a baby Mother put Sister in my carriage and I was supposed to walk. Instead I screamed all the way down the street, "It's my quadge — my quadge." Get it?

JOHN

I get it.

PHILLIP

My can, my barn, my wife, my quadge.

MOLLIE

Don't act ugly, Phillip.

PHILLIP

I feel ugly. I hear ugly songs and see ugly visions.

MOLLIE

Don't blame us, Phillip.

PHILLIP

Who's us?

MOLLIE
John and me.

JOHN
I want to marry Mollie.

PHILLIP
Well, twitch my twiddy. Have you two slept together?

MOLLIE
No, we have not slept together.

PHILLIP
Aren't you going to sleep with him first to find out?

MOLLIE
To find out what?

PHILLIP
If he's as good as me in the nighttime, Butterduck.

MOLLIE
Please, Phillip.

PHILLIP
Please, Phillip. You sound so prissy.

MOLLIE
Me prissy?

PHILLIP
You used to like it in a car, in ditches, in open fields.

MOLLIE
I never liked it in ditches.

JOHN
Don't mind me. Don't mind me.

PHILLIP
I'm not minding you. You come before me like a gnat.

MOLLIE
John was a champion boxer in high school.

PHILLIP
Oh, a tough guy — in high school.

MOLLIE
John was in the Navy for four years.

PHILLIP
And a hero, too.

JOHN
No particular hero. We trained to land on beachheads and slip into secret, dangerous, vulnerable places.

MOLLIE
Sounds downright sexy, John.

PHILLIP
What did you do when you reached those dangerous, secret, vulnerable places?

JOHN
We fought.

MOLLIE
Phillip was in the Army — for only a short time.

JOHN
What happened? Were you wounded?

MOLLIE
Oh no, of course not! He got the mumps.

PHILLIP
I got the mumps and married Mollie.

MOLLIE
What a combination of ideas.

PHILLIP
And I retreated to the most dangerous, secret, vulnerable place of all.

JOHN
No doubt some bar and grill.

MOLLIE
It was the Four Leaf Clover Bar and Grill in Brooklyn Heights.

PHILLIP
That's where, bub. Where's the applejack, Mollie?

MOLLIE
Should you, Phillip?

PHILLIP
Damn well right. I distilled it myself. Three hundred gallons of it. Could have made a fortune with this apple farm. Where is it?

MOLLIE
I drank it.

PHILLIP
Three hundred gallons?

(*He exits into kitchen.*)

MOLLIE
I hid it, but if anybody can find it, he can.

(PARIS *enters.*)

PARIS
What's for dinner?

MOLLIE
We're having cranberry juice cocktails, ham-hocks and greens, and snowball pudding.

PARIS
Ham-hocks and greens, that is my death test. If you wave a plate of ham-hocks and greens over my nose and I don't stir, just nail down the coffin because then you'll know I'm truly dead.

MOLLIE
When Paris was born I craved ham-hocks and greens. It was what they call a difficult confinement.

PARIS
John, can you play chess?

MOLLIE
I was screaming for eight solid hours. And when I was too tired to scream everything got on my nerves so.

PARIS
My grandfather carved it. It's very intricate.

MOLLIE

There were golden and dark shadows lapping up and down the walls like waves. Mother Lovejoy had twisted the funny paper over the light bulb. And I hurt so and the whole room hurt. It was agony — and then —

PARIS

Don't Mother, I can't bear it.

MOLLIE

The agony part is all over, Lambie, you mustn't be so tender-hearted.

PARIS

I am not tenderhearted. It just embarrasses me.

MOLLIE

Embarrasses you?

PARIS

Embarrasses me! Don't you understand? When I hear the words agony or labor, it makes me scrooch up my behind.

MOLLIE

But it was me, Paris. It really happened to me.

PARIS

That doesn't make any difference. It still embarrasses me.

MOLLIE

It happened to you too, Paris Lovejoy, never forget that. Phillip was wonderfully brave. He just sat in a chair across the room drinking Four Roses.

PARIS

The King can only move one square, and the Queen can move anywhere — Why is that?

JOHN

Because the Queen is defending the King. And the King is the point of the game.

PARIS

I know that's the point of the game. When the King is dead, the game is all over.

MOLLIE

When it was all over, Mother Lovejoy cooked a lovely ham-hocks and greens dinner with cornsticks. I couldn't eat any, but Paris knew what he wanted as soon as he touched my breast.

PARIS

Hush up, Mother!

JOHN

That's enough, Mollie.

MOLLIE

Instinct, of course. But it seemed to me a miracle.

PARIS

I'm jumping out of my skin.

(*He exits.*)

JOHN

Mollie, why was Paris named Paris?

MOLLIE

You asked me and I'll tell you. It was inevitable. Phillip and I were on our way to Richmond, staying overnight at the Stratford Arms Motel, to be with Mother Lovejoy until the confinement. Mother Lovejoy had already named him Phillip Ralston Lovejoy IV.

JOHN

Yes, I think the IV is very aristocratic. I get the point.

MOLLIE

Phillip was standing naked at the motel window — the morning sunlight on his body — and we were talking about Paris and how we were going to go there. I was thinking I would be mighty glad to go abroad and get away from Mother Lovejoy.

JOHN

Getting away from Mother Lovejoy is understandable.

MOLLIE

When I was looking at Phillip in the sunlight at the window — suddenly I had the most marvelous unheard-of feeling come over me. It was blissful — something between a fishtail and a ghost — and when I felt it, I cried "Phillip." Phillip turned to me, and I said, "Phillip, no matter whether it's a boy or a girl his name is Paris." And Phillip looked at me a long time and said, "What?"

JOHN

Well, that's a reasonable question.

MOLLIE

But once having named my child, it hurts a mother's heart.

(*We hear sound of guitar.* MOTHER LOVEJOY *enters.*)

MOTHER LOVEJOY

Paris has learned the guitar.

MOLLIE

Without any lessons.

MOTHER LOVEJOY

So I hear. He's not musical the way I used to think of it. At least not like Paderewski. How well I remember Paderewski. I went with Miss Birdie Grimes to hear him play in Atlanta. Birdie Grimes and eighteen other girls, all different ages. We stayed at the Henry Clay Hotel for one day, all of us in one room.

JOHN

That must have been an interesting experience.

MOTHER LOVEJOY

I do like Poles very much, if they're aristocratic and if they're Paderewski. He was such a thrilling man, and so gracious. Shook hands with all of the eighteen pupils, as well as the other three thousand people there. Had a little fur collar on his coat. Through the years every time Paderewski came through Atlanta, I went to hear him. It was a concert of Paderewski's after I married Mr. Lovejoy that started Phillip.

JOHN

How do you mean, started?

MOTHER LOVEJOY

I was sitting there listening to the concert, you know the part that goes dum-da-dum — not that I was able to dance then. I was in the fifth month. And then suddenly I knew.

JOHN

What did you know?

MOTHER LOVEJOY

I knew that my child was going to be a great genius. Premonitions like that are uncanny with a mother. When Loreena was coming I was just nauseated. Let prenatal influence go.

MOLLIE

Where is Sister?

MOTHER LOVEJOY

I ask you, where is Sister. She sits there moping, her nose in a book. If she hadn't strained her eye so much, she wouldn't have been afflicted with those awful spectacles. Her nose is grown to a book. Loreena Lovejoy is hard stock.

MOLLIE

What do you mean?

MOTHER LOVEJOY

Your father was a merchant — you ought to know. The things that are hard to sell. The dry goods and notions store was full of them. That's all he had to sell. Everything from chewing tobacco to chamber pots. That was a store that was all hard stock. No wonder your father got bankrupt. Fort Lee, the Army camp, carried away all the hard stock except Loreena — human hard stock, I mean.

(PHILLIP *enters, carrying the applejack.*)

PHILLIP

Found it. Anybody like a drink?

MOLLIE

Dinner is almost ready.

(*Exits.* MOTHER LOVEJOY *goes right on talking.*)

MOTHER LOVEJOY

I had set my cap on General Slade, who opened the ball at the cotillion, and they say ate eleven pieces of fried chicken. But what happened to my dreams? The Army opens a great career for a woman. But Loreena — she just let the war go by.

PHILLIP (*As he begins pouring a drink*)
Leave Sister alone.

MOTHER LOVEJOY

As you well know, I have never been a bossy mother.

PHILLIP

As I well know, Mother.

MOTHER LOVEJOY

I let my children lead their own lives. True, at first I wanted you to be President, but I'm satisfied that you're a genius.

PHILLIP

I think I would have made a dreamy President.

MOTHER LOVEJOY

Sister — I wanted her to be an opera singer. I said, "Sister, it's all right with me if you sing in grand opera at the Metropolitan." But would she sing at the Metropolitan, would she?

PHILLIP

Leave her alone, Mother.

MOTHER LOVEJOY

Disappointed about grand opera, I said, "Very well, miss, flute and fly." But would she fly? Would she?

PHILLIP

She can't Mother.

MOTHER LOVEJOY (*Asking John*)
Would she flute?

JOHN
I don't know, Mrs. Lovejoy.

MOTHER LOVEJOY
No sir-ree bob. Nothing but tribulations.

(MOTHER LOVEJOY *exits upstairs.*)

PHILLIP
While we are alone, Tucker, I want to tell you I'm glad you
understand Mollie. She is a very special person, and she
needed a special person at a special time.

JOHN
Why are you telling me all this, Lovejoy?

PHILLIP
Because I want you to understand Mollie. She is a poet.

JOHN
A poet?

PHILLIP
Surely you have seen there is a whole ambience of poetry
around her? Clarity, harmony, radiance — that's poetry.
That's Mollie. She is clear as a glass of water, harmonious as
a church organ, and the evening star is not as radiant as Mollie.
You like making poems, Tucker?

JOHN
I never made one.

PHILLIP

You have noticed that logic of absurdity in Mollie. That non sequitur that puts the image over slam-bang. The dichotomies of poetry.

JOHN

What are the dichotomies of poetry?

PHILLIP

Well, heat and cold used almost simultaneously. Sweet and sour.

JOHN

Do you write poetry too?

PHILLIP

Everybody writes poetry when they are in love.

JOHN

Even so, I never wrote any poetry. I tried when I was a kid, but when a line ended with "moon" the next line always came up "June." Kind of obvious.

PHILLIP

That's the main thing about Mollie. There is nothing obvious about her. There is only poetry and understanding. Last night when I lay in bed with her —

JOHN

Mollie slept with you last night?

PHILLIP

Yes and Mollie will never leave me.

JOHN
What makes you so sure?

PHILLIP
Because I am weak, that's why I'm so sure.

JOHN
I never knew a man before, not even a bastard, to glory in his weakness.

PHILLIP
I don't glory in it. I just use it.

JOHN (*Calls*)
Mollie.

(MOLLIE *enters.*)

JOHN
Is it true, Mollie?

MOLLIE
Is what true?

JOHN
Phillip has told me you went to him last night.

PHILLIP
Answer him, Mollie. The man's asked a question.

MOLLIE
If I did something and I'm ashamed, would you forgive me? As if I were drunk.

PHILLIP
You never drink.

MOLLIE

As if I were drugged or somehow powerless. Could you forgive?

JOHN

No.

MOLLIE

And if I tell you it would never happen again so long as we both are alive — would you believe me?

JOHN

No. Why did you do it. Do you still love him?

MOLLIE

No.

JOHN

Is it just pity?

MOLLIE

"Just" is too small a word for pity. It's like saying just food, just God. And whatever my feelings once were for Phillip they were never small. But now it's over. Can't you believe? Can't you forgive?

JOHN

With you Mollie it's better to be miserable and stay as you are than to be deliriously happy if you have to change. When will you be strong enough to love the strong?

MOLLIE

When I look at you I am.

JOHN

When I look at you I can't stand it.

(*He exits.*)

MOLLIE
I want to leave with him.

PHILLIP
I wouldn't try.

(MOLLIE *exits after John.* MOTHER LOVEJOY *comes down the stairs in garden hat and gloves. She is singing.*)

MOTHER LOVEJOY
"I wandered today through the hills, Maggie."

(*She looks at Phillip.*)

What do you look like that for? Your face all screwed up. What is wrong with you, son?

PHILLIP
Mother, have you ever in anguish or acute shame, or terrible embarrassment, subconsciously called a person's name. Have you ever, in the bottom layer of your soul, without words, called someone for help?

MOTHER LOVEJOY
Who would I call?

PHILLIP
I don't know. My father, maybe.

MOTHER LOVEJOY
Your father has been dead to us for many years. But this

has happened to me. Once Patricia Flanoy was talking to me about a dress and I was watching the curtain, in the sewing room, and suddenly the curtain was blown by the wind and the creepiest feeling came over me. It seemed to me that I had seen that curtain blow in the wind, at exactly the same time and heard Patricia Flanoy's voice, "Cut on the bias, Ophelia." The same words, the same curtain, moving in the same wind.

PHILLIP

That's just *déja vu*. A trick of memory.

MOTHER LOVEJOY

It made my flesh crawl.

PHILLIP

A trick of memory.

MOTHER LOVEJOY

You were always a complicated child, Phillip. An eleven-month-old baby just lying there and kicking until I was wild with impatience, wild with waiting.

PHILLIP

I didn't want to be born. I was afraid even then.

MOTHER LOVEJOY

Afraid, nothing. You crawled before any other child, walked before any other child, talked before any other child. When you were eighteen months old, you took up the American flag and walked around the block singing the Marseillaise, "To arms, to arms, you brave . . ."

PHILLIP

Don't, Mother.

MOTHER LOVEJOY

It was practically scary. A little boy in diapers singing the Marseillaise, and marching around the block. I never knew what got into you, or what's the matter with you now.

PHILLIP

Nothing, Mother. Nothing.

MOTHER LOVEJOY

You're not the only soul that suffers. When your father took French leave of us, I had a hard row to hoe. After the shock I had to fall back on my needle. I sewed christening robes, ball dresses, barbecue outfits, shrouds. Sometimes I would sew all day. And I would sing as I sewed:

"Way down yonder in Argentine
A wild cat jumped on a sewing machine
Sewed forty-nine stitches
In a wild cat's britches."

That's sewing some.

PHILLIP

Then Uncle Willie left you all that money.

MOTHER LOVEJOY

Such a fair will. I wanted to send you to music school. You remember how you used to play that Rachmaninoff piece about Moscow burning.

(*She sings.*)

Dum-dum-dum-dum — But no, you were going to be a writer. A writer! Whoever heard of anybody just becoming a writer? I answer notes and letters and R.S.V.P. But just to sit there all day writing something that actually didn't happen. Writing stories and poems that were always sent back to you.

PHILLIP
Except two poems — ten dollars. And one story — twenty.

MOTHER LOVEJOY
I said to you, Son, "Why don't you do something that will fetch you something?"

PHILLIP
You certainly did, Mother.

MOTHER LOVEJOY
Like taking that job I got you in the Feed and Guano Store. But would you work in the Feed and Guano Store? No.

PHILLIP
I was writing.

MOTHER LOVEJOY
I would take those chocolate cupcakes and lemonade out to you in the summerhouse before you discovered beer and spoiled your sweet tooth. I had faith in you all the time whether you were Paderewski or not. Such faith. Even when Birdie Grimes and Patricia Flanoy said you were lazy or crazy or just like your father. When you become famous they had to laugh out of the other side of their mouths. And so did I.

PHILLIP
Then what happened to me, Mother?

MOTHER LOVEJOY
You married Mollie. And she set you down, so you could just work and be idle for ever.

PHILLIP

Mother, tell me, how can you work and be idle for ever?

MOTHER LOVEJOY

After that great success everybody was waiting, Birdie Grimes, Patricia Flanoy, Baby Gozart. The old crowd. The whole world was waiting.

PHILLIP

I tried, Mother. I tried.

MOTHER LOVEJOY

And it was like the mouse and the mountain. The mountain was in labor and the crowds came to watch and see what would be born. And after much rumbling and heaving, the mountain brought forth a mouse.

(SISTER *enters*.)

PHILLIP

Shut up, you babbling old horror.

SISTER

Phillip, how can you talk to Mother like that?

MOTHER LOVEJOY

My ears, do I hear them?

SISTER

Apologize to her.

MOTHER LOVEJOY

Did I hear my ears? Never have I been so mortified.

SISTER

You mortify everybody else, Mother.

MOTHER LOVEJOY
What was it you called me, Phillip?

PHILLIP
I don't remember.

MOTHER LOVEJOY
I do. It's seared in my brain. You called me a babbling old horror. Brooks babble, belles babble, Southern belles. Why, it's their stock in trade. And it's been your stock in trade too, Mr. Phillip Lovejoy. What else have you been doing but babbling. Writing the stories I told you about my Uncle Willie and Birdie Grimes. If you had written about them in an amusing lucrative way like *Gone with the Wind*, that would be different.

PHILLIP
I never wrote about Birdie Grimes.

MOTHER LOVEJOY
You wrote about a little boy on the back fence, and the chinaberry tree and Uncle Willie for six hundred pages, and nothing happened. Absolutely nothing happened.

PHILLIP
He died at the end.

MOTHER LOVEJOY
But it was *my* Uncle Willie.

PHILLIP
Yes, Mother.

MOTHER LOVEJOY
These total recall and total insignificance novels. Why didn't

you ever write something even semicommercial? Look at that little French girl.

PHILLIP

Yes, Mother.

MOTHER LOVEJOY

Babbling old horror . . . and old, who made me old? I'll tell you, Mr. Lovejoy — you and Loreena. And horror! How could you, Phillip? It's not so much the word itself — but the combination — babbling old horror. It will ring in my ears till doomsday. Retract!

SISTER

When family people quarrel among themselves, they know how to wound. Like you pick a piece of material. You know just how to feel it.

PHILLIP

I retract.

MOTHER LOVEJOY

My son, why do you hate me so?

PHILLIP

Because I hate myself.

MOTHER LOVEJOY

I was proud of you — and to anyone who would listen, I boasted — to people on street cars and buses everywhere. But I have a temper too, when I am hurt.

PHILLIP

I haven't noticed your temper, just your bitchiness.

MOTHER LOVEJOY

See! Hear! Never again am I going to finance you and your ugliness. You know what that sanatorium cost?

PHILLIP

Yes.

MOTHER LOVEJOY

Sanatoriums or any other jim-crack foolery, that's final. No more rest homes — *insane* rest homes.

PHILLIP

All right with me.

MOTHER LOVEJOY

And I'm leaving now.

PHILLIP

That's all right too.

MOTHER LOVEJOY

I'm going upstairs, Loreena. After what I've heard in this house, I couldn't stay another minute. Come, Loreena.

(MOTHER LOVEJOY *exits.* SISTER *remains on stage.*)

PHILLIP

I don't know why — I don't know why I want to say I'm sorry — Do I have to tell you what I've gone through these last years?

SISTER

I know, Phillip.

PHILLIP

Fourteen years ago *The Chinaberry Tree* was called a work of genius. Won all the prizes and made a fortune.

SISTER

Phillip, how did you run through all that money?

PHILLIP

Because I didn't believe the money or the fame was real.

SISTER

It was real.

PHILLIP

Real for then, I was right to distrust it. What happened to me?

SISTER

I don't know. I don't know.

PHILLIP

I only know it happened so gradually I didn't even notice it. Other people were aware of it long before I was. Sister, why didn't you tell me?

SISTER

How could I tell you?

PHILLIP

When you saw me drink three martinis before lunch why didn't you slap them from my hand?

SISTER

How could I?

PHILLIP

When I roamed all over the world year after year why didn't you ask me where I was going?

SISTER

Because I didn't know where you wanted to go.

PHILLIP

When I was playing around with other women while Mollie was here, why didn't you give me hell?

SISTER

I did a couple of times, but you don't remember.

PHILLIP

I wish I had not written that goddamn book. I will never forget one day the month that book was published.

SISTER

What happened?

PHILLIP

Nothing. It was just an hour of desolation. I thought that I could never do it again and I was desolate and terrified.

SISTER

All writers when they finish their book think they can never write another.

PHILLIP

For a year, two years, three years, I was afraid to write anything and then when I finished my second book what a clobbering I got.

SISTER

The critics had it in for you. I remember I tore up the reviews and stomped on them.

PHILLIP

Nothing was low enough to say about my second book as nothing was good enough to say about the first. What had happened to me? I kept wondering what had I done?

SISTER

I told you not to take it so hard.

PHILLIP

In the old days I used to admire writers. Now the more writers I know, the less I respect them . . . Three-quarters are homosexuals and the others are rotten in one way or another. They would steal a blind man's stick for a prize or the cover of *Time* Magazine — jealous, trivial, trying to shape their work so that it might go over best and agree with the Code.

SISTER

What code?

PHILLIP

The code of silence. The code of gold.

SISTER

How can you talk that way about writers?

PHILLIP

Because I am a writer and I know. But I used to be a good person. When I was young I used to *like* it when my friends succeeded. I'd clip out the good reviews and the bad reviews I didn't even notice. But now, after these times of fallowness and failure, the only thing that really heartens me is to read of someone else's gut-tearing failure. I feed on the failures of others because I can no longer succeed. The first thing I read in the newspapers each morning are the obituaries. My talent is gone.

SISTER

Where has it gone?

PHILLIP

Where did it come from in the first place? Not from the brain . . .

SISTER

Then where, Phillip?

PHILLIP

From some strange little motor in the soul. And now the motor has stopped.

SISTER

It will start again.

PHILLIP

I've tried to work. Lying up, standing down. I even worked standing at the refrigerator.

SISTER

What for?

PHILLIP

Because Thomas Wolfe did.

SISTER

Did it work?

PHILLIP

No. I just kept opening the refrigerator door and eating. If I had only died the day *The Chinaberry Tree* had come out.

SISTER

That should have been the greatest day of your life.

PHILLIP

If I had suddenly that day been struck by polio or lightning or something out of my control . . .

SISTER

How can you say that, Phillip?

PHILLIP

If I had been suddenly crippled so I was not responsible for the years that lay ahead, but I was responsible for all those years, the slow ruin, the failure. It was I who did it myself, although it happened so slowly, I didn't realize it myself. Only I am responsible for my failure. I and only I.

(MOLLIE *enters.*)

MOLLIE

I want to speak to you, Phillip.

PHILLIP

Speak ahead.

MOLLIE

There's something I want to say.

PHILLIP

Then say it.

SISTER

I'll go upstairs and pacify Mother.

(*Exits up.*)

MOLLIE

I'm going to leave you, Phillip.

PHILLIP

Why?

MOLLIE

Because of John.

PHILLIP

That house builder! You'd be bored with him in twenty-four hours.

MOLLIE

I'd never be bored with him. John and I love each other, and John was going to build us a beautiful house with hot-water pipes running across the floor.

PHILLIP

You would break your neck.

MOLLIE

Not running across the floor. Underneath the floor, I mean. A beautiful house, all new, all shining.

PHILLIP

I need you. You need me. It's as simple as that.

MOLLIE

It's not that simple.

PHILLIP
Do you want me to die?

MOLLIE
No, Phillip, no.

PHILLIP
Well, without you I will die. Don't you understand that?

MOLLIE
No.

PHILLIP
Remember the Stratford Arms Motel when we made love from dawn to noon?

MOLLIE
Stop.

PHILLIP
And you were lying on the bed, buck naked.

MOLLIE
Please, for God's sakes, Phillip.

PHILLIP
And I was standing naked in the open doorway. Suddenly, you cried out — and said, Paris. The name is —

MOLLIE (*Passionately*)
In the name of decency and kindness, keep Paris out of this.

PHILLIP
What in the name of Christ does decency have to do with us?

MOLLIE

Let me go.

PHILLIP

I am weak and you are suddenly strong. Why?

MOLLIE

Because I love again.

PHILLIP

You can't leave me. You have to love me.

MOLLIE

When I was a child I could still live with you. You could beat me and I could still love you the next day. We have been like children, Phillip, primitive like children. Sexy, sure, but primitive like children.

PHILLIP

Remember the Peach Festival.

MOLLIE

I don't want to.

PHILLIP

But you must.

MOLLIE

No.

PHILLIP

The pulse of the festival. The drums and the trumpets. The desire.

MOLLIE

I don't. I don't want to remember.

PHILLIP

Remember the briar patch.

MOLLIE

No, Phillip, no.

PHILLIP

And the bed of moss I made for us after.

MOLLIE

I remember everything. I remember the dead confetti, the thrown-away tin horns. The dawn of the morning after the festival. My rhinestone tiara was broken. My dress torn.

PHILLIP

It was our wedding day.

MOLLIE

A long time ago — when I was still a child.

PHILLIP

How you bawled and kicked before I married you.

MOLLIE (*Looks hard at Phillip.*)

I remember the festival and everything. I remember every time you beat me, every time I cried.

PHILLIP

That was our love, Mollie, the long desire — the romps and tickles —

MOLLIE

I remember everything. But now it's finished.

PHILLIP

You're not going away from me. You love me, Mollie, and
I've got to have you.

(PHILLIP *tries to take Mollie. Rips her blouse.*)

MOLLIE

Let me go, Phillip, let me go.

PHILLIP

This is the showdown —

(*He grabs her.* MOLLIE *picks up knife from dinner
table.* SISTER *enters unnoticed.*)

Go on, Mollie. You're trembling.

MOLLIE

You're mad, Phillip.

PHILLIP

It was you who picked up the knife.

(MOLLIE *hands him the knife.*)

SISTER

Brother — come with me.

PHILLIP

Button your dress, Mollie.

SISTER

Come back, Brother.

PHILLIP

Come back where?

SISTER

Back home. And you can write in the summerhouse.

PHILLIP

Back where I started?

SISTER

Remember the June bugs we flew with strings? The shadows in the summerhouse?

PHILLIP

Once we thought there was a ghost in the summerhouse. Our ghost.

SISTER

Yes. The ghost who made ghost tea parties for us. Mud pies and honeysuckle stew.

PHILLIP

Dandelion sandwiches.

SISTER

And we would dress up in Mother's shoes and hats, and I would put rouge on both of us. Remember the Spanish shawl we always quarreled about?

PHILLIP

And the duets we played. The "Turkish March" and the "Dead March" from *Saul*.

SISTER

And the summer at the shore when we gave a concert.

PHILLIP

We shivered the gizzards of all musicians and made the audience feel queer.

SISTER

Tinny and terrible.

PHILLIP

Ocean pianos are always going out of tune.

SISTER

You were a tranquil child those years.

PHILLIP

But when I grew up and went away, something happened, something shattered.

SISTER

I know.

PHILLIP

Was it alcohol — was it sex that shattered me?

SISTER

Come back with me. Come back to the summerhouse and the shadowed afternoons. You're sick.

PHILLIP

I'm not coming home. You go back with Mother, Sister. And if you can't stand it, drink darling. Just drink in the summerhouse.

(SISTER *exits.*)

Let me stay, Mollie. You can be in love with him, that's all right, but stay in love with me! Let me stay and I will write again.

MOLLIE

I never understood your writing, Phillip.

PHILLIP
It doesn't matter.

MOLLIE
But not understanding it, I loved it even more.

PHILLIP
Don't understand my writing. Understand me.

MOLLIE
It's the same thing.

PHILLIP
Don't you understand, I need you and I can write again. Let me stay.

MOLLIE
No, Phillip.

PHILLIP
We've lived together half our lifetime.

MOLLIE
Since I was fifteen.

PHILLIP
What have I been doing all that time?

MOLLIE
You wrote two books and a play.

PHILLIP
What have you been doing, Mollie?

MOLLIE
Taking care of you, Paris —

PHILLIP

Take care of me now. You have always loved me. Deny that you loved me.

MOLLIE

I don't deny it. I loved you but now it's over.

PHILLIP

There is my old friend again.

MOLLIE

What are you talking about?

PHILLIP

The grandfather, grandfather, grandfather clock. Listen to its tick. Tick-tock, tick-tock. If you leave me, what will happen to all that time?

MOLLIE

What do you mean?

PHILLIP

Don't you know, Mollie, that every moment is a reflection of every moment that has gone before? Without you, there is nothing.

MOLLIE

Please, Phillip.

PHILLIP

And nothing resembles nothing. But nothing is not blank. It is configured hell.

MOLLIE

Let me pass.

PHILLIP

Hell with figures. Don't you see?

MOLLIE

Let me out.

PHILLIP

Noticed clocks on twilight afternoons . . .

MOLLIE

You're drunk, Phillip.

PHILLIP

No. I'm lost. And when you're lost, there is only terror.

MOLLIE

I'm terrified when you talk like this.

PHILLIP

Save me.

MOLLIE

How, Phillip?

PHILLIP

I don't know, but you saved me so many times before.

MOLLIE

I don't know any more.

PHILLIP

This terror, is it of losing you?

MOLLIE

Are you talking about me and you, Phillip? Don't.

PHILLIP

Is it of space? Of time? Or the joined trickery between the two?

MOLLIE

Stop.

PHILLIP

To the lost, all that is in between is agony immobilized.

MOLLIE (*Calls*)

Sister!

PHILLIP

While time, that endless idiot goes screaming around the world.

(MOLLIE *is silent.*)

After all this time. You're not going to leave me.

(*Clock chimes. He looks at Mollie. She is silent. In a fury, he cries out.*)

After all this time . . .

(*He smashes the clock with both hands. He and* MOLLIE *face each other. Both are frightened as clock chimes on and . . .*)

THE CURTAIN FALLS

ACT III, Scene 1

Time: Just before dawn the following day.

At Rise: There is no sound. PHILLIP descends the staircase, slowly, and stands looking at PARIS, who is asleep on the sofa. The following scene is oblique. Neither PHILLIP nor PARIS knows fully what is happening and the intentions of both father and son are veiled, obscure, until PARIS is aware of life and the threat to life.

PHILLIP

Butch —

PARIS

What?

PHILLIP

Wake up, Butch.

PARIS

What time is it?

PHILLIP

Just before dawn. And your mother has packed during the night. She thinks she can leave us.

PARIS

Leave us?

PHILLIP

Yes. Leave me and you.

PARIS

I don't believe you. Why did you wake me?

PHILLIP

Because I need you.

PARIS

How?

PHILLIP

When I was big and you were little you needed me. Don't you remember?

PARIS

I guess so. When I was a baby I would come in and sleep between you and mother. Scared maybe, or I just wanted to. There was a swing somewhere in the neighborhood.

PHILLIP

Where was that?

PARIS

On Cranberry Street. That's as far back as I can remember. How far back can you remember, Daddy?

PHILLIP

I can remember sleeping between my mother and father too.

PARIS

Is that as far back as your memory goes?

PHILLIP

Before that there was only darkness.

PARIS

Darkness?

PHILLIP

Then, years later, there were blazing Georgia afternoons.
Like burning glass, they were.

PARIS

Georgia's hot.

PHILLIP

Hot. Blazing and cruel. July was hot and August longer.

PARIS

Granny has an air-conditioner in her bedroom.

PHILLIP

In those days there were no air-conditioners.

PARIS

What did you do?

PHILLIP

We stewed in the heat.

PARIS

Stewed?

PHILLIP

We squatted in the back yard poking in those doodle-bug
holes. Although I poked at those holes, year in, year out, I
never once saw a doodle bug.

PARIS

What's in those holes?

PHILLIP

That's the mystery. You can squat with a broomstraw all
summer long and never find out.

PARIS

That's no fun.

PHILLIP

I remember as a child picking Spanish bayonets. Remember that bush down South that has sharp spikes, like swords at the end?

PARIS

I had a great time chasing girls with those Spanish bayonets. The girls run and holler. The boys run and chase. Not that you ever jab a girl. They're sharp.

PHILLIP

I jabbed a girl once. Not a hard jab — just a light touch on the behind to make her know I meant business.

PARIS

What did you do after that?

PHILLIP

It was the end of the game.

PARIS

What time is it?

PHILLIP

Time for us to leave.

PARIS

But Mother?

PHILLIP

I told you she's been packing in the night. Silk stockings, brassières, and all that crap.

PARIS
I hate you when you talk like that about Mother.

PHILLIP
What did I say wrong? I love her. I can't live without her.
I have done everything to bring her back to us. I crawled
on the floor like Dostoyevski.

PARIS
Crawled? You didn't care when Mother cried when you
left her.

PHILLIP
I never left her. I did everything and what ever happens to
me it's her fault, and she'll know it. But now we are going
to be at peace. Where I go you and your mother will follow.

PARIS
But where are you going?

PHILLIP
To zones and latitudes you never imagined.

PARIS
In the Arctic Zone the sun shines at midnight. But tell me,
Daddy, where you are going!

PHILLIP
To a place more remote than Kilimanjaro, more vacant than
the moonlight in the Sahara.

PARIS
Africa?

PHILLIP
Not specially.

PARIS

I always wanted to go to Africa. I adore travel and adventure.

PHILLIP

Do you, Butch?

PARIS

When we went to Yellowstone Park I thought it would be an adventure, but the grizzly bears ate out of your hand and slobbered. It was tame. Without your blarney, Daddy, where are you going?

PHILLIP

Do you want me to tell you a story?

PARIS

I feel half asleep and still dreaming.

PHILLIP

In the Kingdom of Heaven . . .

PARIS

What kind of a story is that?

PHILLIP

A Bible story. In the Kingdom of Heaven a man was going to travel to a far-off country. And so he called his two servants —

PARIS

It's funny. The Bible always talks about servants. Mother says to me, "Never say servants, say housekeeper, cleaning maid, or anything — but never servant. Otherwise they quit!"

PHILLIP

The master delivered to the servants his goods —

PARIS
Why did he do that?

PHILLIP
Because he would be gone a long time.

PARIS
What goods did he give them?

PHILLIP
All of his money — his talents.

PARIS
I never thought of talents as money. To me talents mean singing and dancing.

PHILLIP
In the Bible talents are money. It was a way of exchange. Anyway, the master gave five talents to the first servant and to the other just one. And straightway the master left for his journey. Straightway — I love that word. And the one who received five talents traded them with judgment and made ten.

PARIS
On the stock exchange?

PHILLIP
Something like that. For a long time the master stayed away, and when he returned he went to the man who had five talents and the man brought forth five more. "Well done," the master said. "You have used your talents. Enter into the joy of the Lord."

PARIS
You always spend your money. Granny says that if you had

bought stock you would have made a fortune by now. Stocks have gone up.

PHILLIP
Have they, Butch?

PARIS
And you have so many talents, Daddy.

PHILLIP
Then the master went to the servant who had received one talent and the one-talent guy said, "Master, I have hid my talent under the earth — it is still there."

PARIS
Hid it under the earth? Why did he do that?

PHILLIP
Because the master was a hard master and the servant was afraid.

PARIS
What did the master say?

PHILLIP
The master said, "I will take your one talent and give it to the servant who has ten, for to everyone that has, shall be given. But from him that hath not, shall be taken away even that which he has."

PARIS
That's not fair. To me the Bible is nine times out of ten unfair. In fact the Bible is awfully downbeat.

PHILLIP
You're right, Butch. It's not fair.

PARIS

Hattie Brown thinks I have talent. She claims that when I play the guitar I'm as cool as Elvis Presley. When she says that, I wiggle my hips like him — it's nice to have talent.

PHILLIP

It's better to develop it.

PARIS

When I sing like that, Hattie howls.

PHILLIP

Does she, Butch?

PARIS

Why did you wake me up, at this unearthly hour?

PHILLIP

For company.

PARIS

Do you have a hangover, Daddy?

PHILLIP

No.

PARIS

You look white as death.

PHILLIP

I'll be all right, Butch. Once I'm on the road.

PARIS

You should not be going anywhere alone.

(PARIS *starts to dress.*)

PHILLIP

What are you doing?

PARIS

Getting dressed. I ought to go with you.

PHILLIP

It would be company.

PARIS

But where are we going and why are you going? First you said it was Africa. Then you said not. Is it Mexico?

PHILLIP

No.

PARIS

Is it Europe?

PHILLIP

No, Butch.

PARIS

Mother doesn't like Europe. They don't have screens on the windows and you always get the trots.

PHILLIP

It is not Africa, not Mexico, not Europe. No place your mother has ever been or me or you. She thought she could leave us but she can't.

PARIS

Without your baloney, Daddy, what's this all about? Where are you going?

PHILLIP
You'll know when we get there.

PARIS
But Mother?

PHILLIP
I told you forty times she's packing . . .

PARIS
Packing? Tomorrow is the day I was going to try that reel
and tackle. Try it out in the pond. Tomorrow — that is,
today.

PHILLIP
Suppose there are no tomorrows — that is today?

PARIS
What are you doing?

PHILLIP
Getting my books.

PARIS
Why?

PHILLIP
The ancient savage kings gathered their slave, their ship,
their goblet for the voyage.

PARIS
What voyage?

PHILLIP
The last one.

PARIS

You talk so creepy. Strange and downbeat, I'm scared.

PHILLIP

Why are you scared?

PARIS

If I knew why, I would not be so scared.

PHILLIP

It's almost daybreak.

PARIS

I'm wide awake now.

PHILLIP

It's time to get started.

PARIS

I can't go anywhere like this.

(*Indicating his socks*)

The socks don't mate. I have on one white sock and one red.

PHILLIP

Is that the only reason you don't want to come?

PARIS

Not only that.

PHILLIP

I remember the October moons of my childhood. The hound dog would be baying. When there was a ring around the moon it was a sign of coming frost. Have you ever seen frost flowers, Butch? With its cold and delicate designs that come on windowpanes — they are rose-colored and gold.

PARIS

I never saw that.

PHILLIP

I'm not blaming you, Son.

PARIS

Blaming me?

PHILLIP

No. It operates like this. In our cold house where there was no central heating, Uncle Willie used to light the kitchen stove first thing in the morning and put on the grits for break-fast — old people get up very early in the morning. And as the room would warm with the glowing kitchen stove, outside there would still be cold and wintertime. Then the frost flowers would come on the windowpanes. Jack Frost had painted them we always said.

PARIS

This is just the time to dig for angleworms. You find them better just at dawn.

PHILLIP

Or late twilight. I, too, have dug for angleworms.

PARIS

Hattie and I are going to start early. Go to the pond. And if the fish aren't biting there, we'll go to Rockland Lake.

PHILLIP

You won't come with me?

PARIS

My day is important and already planned. Some other time,
Daddy.

PHILLIP

I, too, remember sleeping between my mother and my father
and having chased girls with Spanish bayonets. I have known
both frost flowers and angleworms. And I have known that
time when a song on the street and a voice from childhood
all fitted and I was a writer and writing every day. And I was
not alone then. There was love. I could love and did not
struggle against being loved. It was company, anyhow. I
remember everything — and at that instant will every moment
be a reflection of every moment that has gone before?

(*Almost whispers*)

I can't stand it.

PARIS (*Shouts*)

Mother!

PHILLIP (*Whispers*)

Now I prefer only darkness.

(*He exits.* MOLLIE *enters.*)

MOLLIE

What on earth, Lambie — ?

PARIS

My daddy.

(*We hear the sound of the car.*)

MOLLIE
What about Daddy? Where is he going at this hour?

PARIS
I don't know, Mother. I just don't know.

MOLLIE (*Goes to window, looking after the car.*)
Lambie, please, put down that guitar.

THE CURTAIN FALLS

ACT III, Scene 2

Time: A week later.

At Rise: HATTIE *and* PARIS *enter from kitchen.*

HATTIE
Those funny things on the furniture. Are they for mourning?

PARIS
It's just dust covers because we're leaving tomorrow.

HATTIE
What kind of place is Brooklyn Heights?

PARIS

It's a neighborhood where we used to live. Crumby place, as I remember it.

HATTIE

They are like mourning — so white and strange. Why did your daddy do it?

PARIS

He never did it. It was an accident.

HATTIE

But he drove the car off the road down to the pond, which is a good ways away. Everybody said it was deliberate.

PARIS

I don't care what everybody says. It was not deliberate. It was a defective steering wheel. John explained the whole thing to me.

HATTIE

They say in the village it was suicide.

PARIS

Suicide. It's weak to commit suicide. And my father was a strong man. He once lifted two hundred pounds as though they were dummy weights.

HATTIE

Where?

PARIS

At a fair he took me to one time. My father loved fairs and festivals, commotions.

HATTIE

I was always afraid of your father.

PARIS

Here is a problem. If in the middle of a forest, a tree falls and nobody is there, not a soul in the world for miles around — would there be the sound of a crash?

HATTIE

Well, somebody might have heard.

PARIS

But if nobody, nobody was there, and I mean nobody in the world — would the crash be heard?

HATTIE

Maybe a little animal or a mole or something would hear.

PARIS

A little animal? Of course. Why hadn't I thought of that?

HATTIE

Why are you so strange?

PARIS

I'm not strange, but I saw my father in the coffin at the funeral home.

HATTIE

I wouldn't look at a dead person if you gave me a hundred dollars. Mother says it's morbid to look at dead coffins. How is *your* mother?

PARIS

She just sits there huddled in Daddy's room — as if she were terribly, terribly cold. Granny wants her to break down. Granny breaks down and cries and cries — but Mother just sits there huddled and looking cold. Auntie Sister looks like she's waiting for something.

> HATTIE

I don't think they open coffins at the Episcopal ceremony. Paris, don't act so strange this last afternoon. Aren't we going to kiss goodbye?

> PARIS

You're not supposed to smooch with girls on account of their self-respect.

> HATTIE

You mentioned you were going to give me a present. What is it?

> PARIS

Old costumes and things like that. And my sled. I won't have use for those things in Brooklyn Heights. It's down in the cellar. Let's go down.

> HATTIE

Aren't you really going to kiss me before you go?

> PARIS

I reckon so. But if a tree falls in this absolutely silent forest with no human beings anywhere in the world and *no* animals . . .

> (PARIS *and* HATTIE *exit outside to cellar.* MOTHER LOVEJOY *and* SISTER *come downstairs with assorted suitcases.*)

MOTHER LOVEJOY

Poor Mollie. She hasn't eaten a thing all week, while I have to stuff myself. Grief does that to me.

SISTER

I noticed, Mother.

MOTHER LOVEJOY

The same way when Mr. Lovejoy left. I got stout from so much grief-eating. I made fudge, spludge, divinity and every candy known to man.

SISTER

I just eat normally.

MOTHER LOVEJOY

But then you never loved your brother like we did.

SISTER

What are you saying, Mother?

MOTHER LOVEJOY

You were jealous of him always.

SISTER

But isn't that natural?

MOTHER LOVEJOY

Life is over for us. Mollie just sits there in Phillip's room and she can never love again. Mollie and I are very much alike.

SISTER

I never noticed it.

MOTHER LOVEJOY

When we love, we love once. One man for a lifetime.

SISTER

After a while Mollie will get over it. She is going to get a job and live in New York.

MOTHER LOVEJOY

What kind of job?

SISTER

In a cosmotologist parlor.

MOTHER LOVEJOY

Remember her last job as a cosmotologist, when Phillip left her? Poor woman, bald as an egg.

SISTER

That woman and Mollie are good friends now. They correspond frequently.

MOTHER LOVEJOY

Just the same. Getting a job and living in New York is one thing but having loved a genius is another.

SISTER

What is a genius?

MOTHER LOVEJOY

Genius is, I suppose, something light and dark and lovable and failing, all at the same time.

SISTER

That doesn't make sense.

MOTHER LOVEJOY
Genius is written in the newspapers.

SISTER
So was Al Capone.

MOTHER LOVEJOY
Now that your brother is dead, can't you stop being jealous?

SISTER
Don't you understand, I was never jealous. I would just think about Phillip writing and how he never had to bother about libraries and index cards and books that were overdue. And he never had to keep quiet in the Children's Section. But I was never jealous. I just wanted to be like Phillip was.

MOTHER LOVEJOY
The hired limousine will be here soon.

SISTER
Why did you hire a limousine?

MOTHER LOVEJOY
In a limousine you can weep all the way to the station. Taxi drivers might wonder and question.

SISTER
I like taxi drivers.

MOTHER LOVEJOY
Let's hurry.

SISTER
We still have hours.

MOTHER LOVEJOY

I have to be at the station in plenty of time.

SISTER

Tell me, Mother, have you ever missed a train?

MOTHER LOVEJOY

Mercy no. But then I have always been on time. When I was a young girl I dreamed that I was going to the station to get on a train, and when I looked down I didn't have any clothes on. I was so embarrassed. Standing there, naked. In the dream, of course.

SISTER

Well, you're dressed now.

MOTHER LOVEJOY

Did you pack the lunch?

SISTER

We're having turkey sandwiches.

MOTHER LOVEJOY

I hope you put plenty of mayonnaise on mine. I like them squelchy.

SISTER

I made them squelchy.

(*Car is heard driving up.* MOLLIE *enters from upstairs.*)

MOLLIE

The limousine is coming up the drive.

MOTHER LOVEJOY
Don't cry, Mollie. There's a time for tearin' and a time for mendin' and a time for weepin', and a time for . . . and so forth.

MOLLIE
I'm not crying.

MOTHER LOVEJOY
What was that man doing at the services?

MOLLIE
Which man?

MOTHER LOVEJOY
Your former tenant in the barn.

MOLLIE
John? John Tucker? I don't know.

(*She turns away.*)

MOTHER LOVEJOY (*Only to Mollie*)
Practically a total stranger. And he didn't cry at all. Such bad manners.

(*A pause*)

My son was a great genius. Forever I will speak of my son, in stores and trains and public conveyances and you will too, Mollie.

MOLLIE
Goodbye, Sister. I love you.

SISTER
On my August vacation, I'll come up and stay with you.

MOLLIE
My home is always your home. Although I don't know where it is now.

(PARIS *re-enters*.)

Paris, come say goodbye to Granny and Sister.

MOTHER LOVEJOY
I'm going to make you my beneficiary, Paris.

PARIS
What's that?

MOTHER LOVEJOY
I am going to leave you all my money, except for annuities. Your Auntie Sister should have something to look forward to.

PARIS
You mean I will be rich?

MOTHER LOVEJOY
Never say "rich." Say well-heeled, or comfortable circumstances. But never say "rich," that's vulgar.

PARIS
I am already in comfortable circumstances. How much money is it?

MOTHER LOVEJOY
Paris, they all want to find that out. All the town wants to know. Your mother and aunt ask careful, delicate questions, but I head them off. Well, let's not be sentimental.

PARIS

O.K. Granny.

MOTHER LOVEJOY

And Mollie, although I can't support you in the grandest style, you can always come home to Society City.

MOLLIE

I won't ever come back to Society City.

MOTHER LOVEJOY

If you are crippled or sick or something, it's a comfort to know.

MOLLIE

I just hope I never will be crippled or sick.

MOTHER LOVEJOY

We're going to stay at a hotel in New York tonight. What is that hotel across from the Grand Central Station?

SISTER

The Commodore.

MOTHER LOVEJOY

The Commodore. I adore naval people. Goodbye. Goodbye everybody.

(MOTHER LOVEJOY *and* SISTER *exit.*)

PARIS

Mother, don't cry. Don't be sad, please. What can I do for you, Mother? It makes me sad to see you cry.

MOLLIE

Recite or sing something, Lambie. It always soothes me.

PARIS

You know I can't sing. My voice is changing.

MOLLIE

Say something that suits my nerves and the occasion.

PARIS

What, Mother?

MOLLIE

Recite "The Woman Was Old and Ragged and Gray."

PARIS

Not that poem, Mother.

MOLLIE

And bent with the chill on a winter's day.

PARIS

It's so sad, so blue.

MOLLIE

I'm sad. Desolate, in fact. And old and withered and gray.

PARIS

You only have nine gray hairs, Mother. Nine's not much.

MOLLIE

Bent by the chill. I'm cold. I'm ragged and gray and cold.

PARIS

You are not ragged, Mother or that old, Mother.

MOLLIE

Paris, we need some cord for the boxes.

PARIS
I'll get it.

MOLLIE (*Alone*)
No, I will never be able to speak of Phillip, in stores, in trains, in public conveyances.

(JOHN *is seen standing in the open door.*)

MOLLIE
Why did you come back?

JOHN
To get you and Paris.

MOLLIE
We're not going with you.

JOHN
Why, Mollie?

MOLLIE
Because I was responsible.

JOHN
Responsible for what?

MOLLIE
Phillip's death.

JOHN
How were you responsible?

MOLLIE
Because I loved you, Phillip died.

JOHN
Don't say that.

MOLLIE
I loved you, and he died.

JOHN
Don't even think it.

MOLLIE
I saw him, John.

JOHN
How?

MOLLIE
I had packed in the night, and he saw me packing. When one person leaves another person after fifteen years, and he sees them packing . . . Don't you see how I was responsible?

JOHN
No.

MOLLIE
But I saw him. I came down because Paris called me. It was dawn. The sky was pale blue like a water color that had just been painted and is not yet dry. At that moment I heard the car and watched from the kitchen window as Phillip drove down the road. He stopped and veered the car sideways, catty-cornered in the open fields. And there he stopped the car. I wondered. He must have been sitting there wondering too.

JOHN
What were you wondering?

MOLLIE
I was grieving.

JOHN
What were you grieving about?

MOLLIE
Don't make me tell you now.

JOHN
Tell me.

MOLLIE
The apple blossoms were still against that pale blue sky.

JOHN
What were you grieving about Mollie?

MOLLIE
I was missing you. At that moment before he died, I was missing you. Then Phillip suddenly started the car and, as I was watching, drove into that green summer pond. It was as though he knew what I was thinking. Then I was scream-ing in the road and nobody heard me, it was so silent. Why couldn't I have helped him?

JOHN
You did help him. For half your lifetime you helped him.

MOLLIE
If I had truly helped him, he would be alive today. But I was responsible and so were you. I nursed him, I lived with him, I loved him, for fifteen years, so let me alone, leave me to my grief.

JOHN

What can I say?

MOLLIE

Nothing.

JOHN

All right. You were responsible. You were responsible for keeping life in a man who no longer wanted to live.

(*Enters* PARIS *carrying his space suits.*)

MOLLIE

Phillip was a poet, a wizard of words and sometimes I did not even pay attention to him. You can't say anything, so go.

PARIS

Yes, Daddy could talk. That's how I'll always remember him. Blarney! He woke me up that early morning and he was talking about frost flowers and Africa and heaven and hell.

MOLLIE

Frost flowers? How strange!

(*To John*)

Why, do you suppose?

PARIS

Oh he wanted me to come with him.

MOLLIE (*Horrified*)

To come with him!

(*To John*)

Oh Phillip couldn't. Could he?

JOHN
I don't know.

MOLLIE (*Hugs Paris.*)
I don't think so. I don't think any father could. But why did he want Paris to come? What plan did he have?

JOHN
Maybe none.

MOLLIE
No I'm sure. If he had wanted to take anybody with him that way it would have been me.

(*To Paris*)

But Lambie, I don't want to age you before your time. Look at these lovely apple branches and the sunlight. I wonder if the Salvation Army takes space suits. I have lots of clothes that are just right for the Salvation Army.

JOHN
Mollie, when I was in the Navy, a boy fell overboard and I jumped in and tried to save him. But I could not. In the struggle he kept pulling me down. He kept hitting me until I finally had to let go.

MOLLIE
John come and look at these lovely apple branches and the sunlight.

(*A moment together looking at the apple blossoms and at each other.*)

JOHN

Mollie. How many times do a man and a woman love each other? I mean times from now on? How many times do they see exactly like these apple blossoms and the May morning and the green sky? How many times . . . how many times?

MOLLIE

I guess sometimes you've got to leave some things to God.

JOHN

You are damn well right. You have to leave something to God. Paris, one of these days I am going to marry your mother!

PARIS

Soon. I hope.

JOHN

And I am going to build that house, I told you about.

PARIS

When you were describing it, it sounded wonderful; the square root of it in fact. I will just mosey off now, and read the funny papers.

MOLLIE

John. You must know, I loved Phillip.

JOHN

I know.

MOLLIE

If you hang me by my hair, and twist my elbow, I will still say I *once* loved him.

JOHN

I guess you would, under the circumstances.

MOLLIE

I loved him in the halcyon years when we were young. Is halcyon a word?

JOHN

A word in books.

MOLLIE

I can't write in books about my love for Phillip, but if in the middle of the night you, John Tucker, give me the tiniest meanest little pinch to find out, I would still say I once loved him.

JOHN

In the middle of the night, I think we will have more to do than to give you the tiniest, meanest pinch to find out.

MOLLIE

Still —

JOHN

Still. I still love the ocean and scenery on the shore. I could still make shore dinners of lobsters and clams and seaweed.

MOLLIE

What did Paris mean? The square root of wonderful?

JOHN

Just something I told him in another context.

MOLLIE

But what is the square root of wonderful?

JOHN
You.

MOLLIE
Me? Arithmetic isn't it?

JOHN
That's right, Mollie.

MOLLIE
Does it multiply?

JOHN
No. More like divide.

MOLLIE
Me divide? To me love multiplies. When I fell in love with Phillip I loved everybody.

JOHN
Everybody?

MOLLIE
The manager of the Peach Festival, Tootsie Johnson and Billie Little.

JOHN
Who's Billie Little?

MOLLIE
Just somebody I knew in those far-off days of love. Luminous, you might say, like this table . . . this chair.

JOHN
This table, this chair?

MOLLIE
. . . and when I fell in love with you, John, I loved everybody.

JOHN
Everybody again?

MOLLIE
Phillip. The yardman, Sister, Mother Lovejoy . . .

JOHN
The yardman and Sister are all right. But I would have drawn the line at Mother Lovejoy.

MOLLIE
But don't you understand . . . if I had not loved so much, John, could I love you as I do?

THE CURTAIN FALLS